THE
MIDNIGHT
LIBRARY

—

Voices

THE MIDNIGHT LIBRARY

Voices

Nick Shadow

Hodder
Children's
Books

A division of Hodder Headline Limited

Special thanks to Shaun Hutson

Text copyright © 2005 Working Partners Limited
Illustration copyright © 2005 David McDougall
Created by Working Partners Limited, London W6 0QT

First published in Great Britain in 2005
by Hodder Children's Books

2 4 6 8 10 9 7 5 3 1

A Catalogue record for this book is available from
the British Library

ISBN 0 340 89405 9

Typeset in Weiss Antiqua by Avon DataSet Ltd,
Bidford-on-Avon, Warwickshire

Printed and bound in Great Britain by
Clays Ltd, St Ives plc

The paper and board used in this paperback by
Hodder Children's Books are natural recyclable products
made from wood grown in sustainable forests. The manufacturing
processes conform to the environmental regulations
of the country of origin.

Hodder Children's Books
a division of Hodder Headline Limited
338 Euston Road
London NW1 3BH

Welcome, reader.

My name is Nick Shadow,
curator of that secret
institution:

The Midnight Library

Where is the Midnight Library, you ask?
Why have you never heard of it?
For the sake of your own safety, these questions are better left
unanswered. However ... so long as you promise not to reveal
where you heard the following (no matter who or *what*
demands it of you), I will reveal what I
keep here in the ancient vaults.
After many years of searching,
I have gathered the most terrifying
collection of stories known to
man. They will chill you to
your very core, and make
flesh creep on your young,
brittle bones. Perhaps you should
summon up the courage and turn the
page. After all, what's the worst that
could happen ... ?

M·L

The Midnight Library: Volume I

Stories by Shaun Hutson

CONTENTS

VOICES

The hospital corridor seemed to stretch away into forever as Kate Openshaw and her dad walked slowly along it, their footsteps echoing around them. They had made this walk more times than Kate cared to remember in the three months since her mum had been taken mysteriously ill.

Outside, the rain was pelting against the large windows that overlooked the hospital grounds. Kate shivered.

'Dad,' she said, unable to bear the silence any longer. 'How many more tests will they have to do on Mum?'

'I don't know, Kate,' her dad replied quietly. 'They'll just keep on until they find out what's wrong.'

'But they've been doing tests for *months* now,' Kate protested. 'And they still haven't found anything. Not even when they did that big operation on her throat last week.'

'I know.' Kate's dad slipped a comforting arm around her shoulder. 'But we've got to trust the doctors. They're doing their best.'

There was a large set of double doors ahead. Kate pushed them hard in frustration. They swung back on their hinges and she and her dad passed through into the next stretch of corridor. To Kate, it felt as if the pale walls were somehow closing in, growing more and more narrow. 'I hate this place,' she said as they continued their endless trek.

'No one likes hospitals, Kate,' her dad said gently.

'But you know we've got no choice about coming here. Maybe when the doctors have finished the latest set of tests they'll have a better idea of what to do.'

Kate wasn't sure whether he was trying to reassure her or himself. Probably a bit of both.

The rain was falling even more heavily, whipped by an increasingly strong wind that caused some of the bushes close to the windows to slap their leaves and branches loudly against the glass.

Another set of doors loomed ahead, WARD 6 displayed above them. Kate swallowed hard. Her mum's ward.

She followed her dad through the doors. A few nurses and patients waved to them. Kate waved back. Everyone on the ward was so friendly, and had been ever since her mum had first arrived there.

Kate knew she shouldn't be afraid of coming here but she couldn't help herself. She glanced at some curtains that were drawn around one of the beds to her right and wondered what was going on behind them. Then she decided she would rather not know.

'You OK?' her dad asked, as they approached the two beds at the end of the ward.

Kate nodded.

One of the beds was empty.

The other one was occupied by Kate's mum.

There were two doctors and a nurse standing around the bed. Kate saw that they were all looking very serious.

The older doctor, who Kate knew was called Dr Venner and was in charge of looking after her mum, looked up. Seeing Kate and her dad, he walked over to meet them.

'Has there been a change in my wife's condition, doctor?' Kate's dad asked anxiously.

'I'm very sorry to say that your wife's condition has worsened, Mr Openshaw,' Dr Venner replied quietly.

Kate felt a shiver run through her when she heard the words.

'In all my years as a doctor I've never seen a case like Mrs Openshaw's before,' Dr Venner went on. 'We've tried everything.' He put a sympathetic hand on Kate's shoulder. 'We'll keep trying, but I can't promise anything, I'm afraid,' he said gently.

Kate felt tears welling up in her eyes.

'We'll leave you alone to have some time with her,' Dr Venner finished. He beckoned to the other doctor and the nurse, and the three of them walked slowly away, heads bowed, deep in discussion.

Kate waved at her mum and smiled as bravely as she could. Then she walked over, leaned forward and kissed her cheek. 'How are you feeling, Mum?' she asked, looking at the thick dressing that still covered her mum's throat.

Kate saw her mum's lips move and leaned in closely, as she'd been forced to do since the illness had reduced her mum's voice to a whisper.

'I'm fine, darling,' her mum croaked.

But Kate could see that wasn't true. It wasn't true at all.

Kate's dad sat down at the other side of the bed looking anxious.

Her mum reached up and squeezed his hand before turning her attention back to Kate. 'How are you, darling?' she asked. 'How's school? What have you been doing today?' She gasped, as if the effort of speaking was now even more painful.

'Just the usual stuff, Mum,' Kate replied, holding her mum's hand tightly.

Just then, another doctor came over. Kate could see the man's name badge on his long white coat. Dr Gregory Solomon.

Dr Solomon gazed over the chart hanging at the bottom of the bed, occasionally making a mark with the pen he'd taken from his pocket. Looking even more serious, he asked Kate's dad to go and chat with him in his office.

Kate watched as her dad disappeared through a door halfway down the ward. Then she felt her mum's hand take her own to get her attention. She leaned in closer so that her mum could whisper in her ear.

'Darling, will you do something for me?' her mum said, again having to force the words out in a gasp.

'Of course, Mum,' Kate replied. 'Anything!'

Her mum smiled. It was a sad smile. She lifted her head from the pillow to give Kate a kiss, her lips catching Kate's ear. Then she gave a long sigh. 'It would have been Gran's birthday tomorrow,' she said. 'Could you get some flowers and put them on her grave for me?'

'Sure, Mum.'

'Take the money from my purse in the locker by my bed,' her mum said. 'Get a bouquet of irises if you can. Your gran loved those.'

'OK, Mum,' Kate agreed. 'I can get them from the florist's in the hospital on our way home and take them to the graveyard on my way to school in the morning.'

'Good idea,' her mum gasped. 'I'd rather you did

that than go to the graveyard after school. The evenings draw in pretty quick now and I don't want you wandering about in the dark on your own.'

As she moved back slightly, Kate saw that her mum's eyes held an urgent expression. 'Don't worry, Mum, I usually walk home with Susie,' Kate reassured her.

Then she looked up to see her dad returning from Dr Solomon's office. He looked pale and defeated.

'I love you, Mum,' Kate said, fighting back the tears.

'I love you too,' her mum said, squeezing her hand. 'That's why I'm determined to get better. I don't want to leave you and your dad.'

'Come on, Kate,' her dad said. 'We'd better go, let Mum get some rest.'

Kate kissed her mum and walked back down the ward. She turned and waved, and her mum smiled weakly back.

As she'd promised, Kate visited the hospital florist near the main entrance of the hospital and bought a bunch of irises, and then she and her dad hurried through the rain to the car.

Kate glanced over her shoulder at the hospital as they drove away, the rain still hammering against the windscreen.

Somewhere in the distance there was a low rumble of thunder.

By the following morning, the rain had stopped. Despite a sharp chill in the air, the sun shone brightly, reflecting on the puddles that Kate skirted as she walked along the road that led to the church. The air smelled beautifully fresh and crisp. Early morning dew sparkled on spider webs like diamonds on thin silver chains.

The streets were still relatively quiet; Kate had left earlier than usual, so that she could visit Gran's grave before school. She looked down at the bouquet of irises she'd bought the night before.

Ahead of her, the church spire thrust upwards

towards the clear blue morning sky. Her footsteps crunched on the gravel path as she made her way through the churchyard entrance and along one of the pathways to the area of the graveyard where her gran was buried.

Many of the gravestones near the church were extremely old and Kate slowed down to glance at the wording on them. Some of them were hard to read, the letters worn away by the passage of time. A couple of the oldest-looking stones were so blackened by mildew and mould, they looked like rotting teeth sticking up from the ground.

Kate moved closer to wipe some of the mould away, so that she could read the lettering. As she did so, a fat black slug slid into view on top of the gravestone. Kate wrinkled her nose and quickly drew her hand away. She watched the slug glide slowly down the stonework on its sparkling silver slime trail until it disappeared into the wet grass at the base of the stone.

'You won't find any names on those two headstones.'

The voice startled her and she spun round quickly, standing up.

It was the vicar – Reverend Dodds, who had performed Gran's funeral a few months ago. His priest's collar stood out with brilliant whiteness against the blackness of his robes.

'Sorry if I startled you,' he said, gently.

'It's OK,' Kate replied.

The vicar narrowed his eyes slightly then smiled at her. 'It's Kate Openshaw, isn't it?' he said. 'We met at your gran's funeral.'

Kate smiled and nodded. 'That's why I'm here,' she told him. 'It would have been Gran's birthday today. My mum asked me to put these on her grave.' Kate held up the bouquet of irises.

'What a lovely thought,' said Reverend Dodds. 'I won't keep you, then.'

Kate was about to continue on her way, but then paused and looked back at the two cracked and mouldy headstones she'd been inspecting before Reverend Dodds appeared. 'You said I wouldn't find any names on these two gravestones,' she said. 'Why not? I know they're very old but . . .'

'It wasn't the weather or the time that caused the damage to the stones. It was other people,' replied Reverend Dodds.

Kate looked up at him, puzzled.

Reverend Dodds grinned. 'You'll have to forgive me, Kate, but I can be quite a bore on this subject. I've been studying the history of this church since I arrived here a few years ago. Those two graves are over three hundred years old. They belong to a mother and daughter who were believed by some parishioners to be witches. The vicar of the time dismissed these claims and allowed the women to be buried here on church ground. But the parishioners who disagreed with him scratched the women's names from their headstones.'

Kate shivered. 'Those poor women. I'm on the vicar's side. I don't believe in witches.'

'Not even the broomstick-riding kind?' Reverend Dodds asked, smiling.

Kate grinned back and shook her head.

'Many of those accused of witchcraft were executed in those days, you know,' Reverend Dodds went on. 'It was often because they seemed able to foresee the future. Those who executed them said they'd been given the power by the Devil, so must be witches.'

'It doesn't seem to be such a bad thing to be able to tell the future,' Kate remarked. 'You'd know about things before they happened. Like which numbers would win the lottery!'

Reverend Dodds smiled. 'Well, in times gone by, that kind of ability would have got you burned at the stake as a witch.' He looked down at the two ancient, weathered gravestones, his tone darkening a little. 'Anyone who lived alone, who wasn't liked by others or who was a little unusual, they were all likely to be accused of being a witch. No one was safe.'

Kate nodded.

'Anyway, I'll leave you to get on with what you were doing,' Reverend Dodds said, and he turned to walk back towards the church.

Kate watched him disappear inside, then walked briskly along the gravel path to her gran's grave.

'Hello, Gran,' she said softly, kneeling beside the headstone. 'Happy birthday.' She wiped some fallen leaves from the base of the marble headstone and laid the bouquet of irises there. 'I brought these for you, from me and Mum. I know they were your favourites.' Somehow, it seemed natural, to be speaking to Gran like this. 'Mum can't come herself as she's still really ill in hospital, Gran,' Kate went on. 'The doctors still can't find what's wrong with her. I hope that you're watching her, keeping her safe. Wherever you are, Gran, I hope you're listening and that you're OK.'

'I'm fine thanks, love.'

Kate spun round, looking for the voice that had

whispered into her ear – so close she could have sworn she felt the breath.

The graveyard was still empty apart from herself.

She looked back down at her gran's gravestone and swallowed hard. 'Gran?' she said uncertainly. 'Gran, is that you?'

A slight breeze ruffled the hair around the back of her neck. It felt like the soft touch of a hand.

Kate looked round again, but there was no one to be seen. The skin on her arms rose into goose bumps. The cellophane that the bouquet of irises was wrapped in crackled in the wind.

She rose to her feet and then backed away, almost stumbling on to the path.

'Oh, I wish I'd been able to be there! Describe it to me.'

'Well, as Aunt Augustine requested, everyone was wearing purple and white. And you should have seen the way they'd made those flowers spell out her name. It was beautiful. They'd really done her proud.'

Again Kate looked around. No one could be seen.

Where were these voices coming from? Her heart was thudding against her ribs now.

Kate hurriedly made her way towards the church gate. As she passed the church, the voices seemed to grow louder.

'It was absolutely beautiful. It really was the most beautiful funeral I've ever been to. Just what Aunt Augustine would have wanted . . .'

Kate sighed to herself in relief. A funeral service must have started inside. The church was old. Its ceiling was high. The sound of voices in there would carry.

Kate nodded to herself. That must be it. Mystery solved.

She headed on towards the gate.

'I'm sure Aunt Augustine would have been watching. She'd have been looking down on it all and smiling.'

'Especially when she heard her favourite hymn being played at the end. She always loved "The Old Rugged Cross" . . .'

The voices were growing fainter again.

Kate left the churchyard and hurried on down the

road towards school, a cold breeze whipping her hair around her face.

That day at school passed the same as every other: a few laughs with Susie and her other friends, a couple of arguments with some of the boys in her class. Talk of what they'd watched on TV the night before. What they were going to do at the weekend.

The only downside had been Daisy Barton, as usual – who had told Susie she had a spare WestZone CD that Susie could buy for half-price. WestZone was everyone's favourite band at the moment, and this was the only WestZone CD that Susie didn't have.

'She never told me it had a dirty great scratch across it,' Susie complained, as the two girls sat at the back of the class. 'I didn't realize until after I'd paid her for it and tried to play it at home last night. And she wouldn't take it back. She's always doing things like that to people.'

'Daisy only cares about herself,' Kate replied. 'And

she's probably jealous that you managed to get a ticket for the WestZone concert and she didn't because she was too lazy to get to the box-office and queue for hours like we did.'

Susie smiled. 'You're probably right,' she said, looking more cheerful.

'I've got to nip down the shops on the way home,' Susie told Kate when the final bell went. 'Do you want to come?'

'I'd better get home,' Kate replied. 'I usually get Dad's tea ready before we go and see Mum in hospital.'

'OK, give your mum my love, Kate,' Susie said, and she rushed off in the opposite direction.

Kate stood alone for a moment then set off in the direction of home. It was getting dark already as she passed the church.

'Tell him I want those photos by Friday or I'm not paying.'

Kate slowed her pace, the voice loud in her ear.

'*I've told him, but he says there's nothing he can do about it.*'

The tone of the argument was growing more heated. Kate found herself wandering closer to the open church door.

'*I'm not going to tell you again, I want them Friday, or I'm not paying.*'

She poked her head around to see what was going on.

The church was empty.

'*Do what you like. I've spoken to him and that's all I can do.*'

Confused, Kate couldn't work out where the words were coming from. She took a couple of steps inside the building, glancing at the beautifully coloured stained-glass windows.

'Hello, Kate.'

She spun round, startled – but this time it was a familiar voice.

Reverend Dodds was standing close behind the door, pinning something to the notice-board there.

'Sorry if I made you jump,' he said, cheerfully. 'Can I help you?'

'I heard someone talking,' Kate said, falteringly. 'In here.'

'Not unless you heard me talking to myself,' he smiled. 'And I hope you didn't, they say that's the first sign of madness, don't they?'

Kate nodded, looking around the church again, the other voices still echoing inside her head. She was sure that the argument had come from inside the church. 'Sorry to have disturbed you,' she said. Then she turned and quickly left.

Kate sat beside her mum's bed. She couldn't stop smiling. Her mum was sitting up, looking better than Kate had seen her for months.

Dr Venner glanced at the chart he held and shook his head, a smile playing on his lips. 'I must say, your mum is a constant puzzle to us, Kate,' he began. 'First she comes into the hospital and we can't find out what's wrong with her, and then she suddenly begins to recover and we don't know why. I must say, the improvement is remarkable.'

'Does that mean she can come home?' Kate asked.

'Hopefully,' Dr Venner said. 'But let's just see what happens, shall we? You want your mum back to her old self, don't you? And we certainly don't want her leaving here until she is.'

He replaced the chart, smiled at them all and turned in the direction of another patient further down the ward.

'Happier now?' Kate's dad asked her.

Kate nodded and smiled. 'Do you really feel better, Mum?' she asked.

'Much better,' her mum said quietly, reaching out to squeeze Kate's hand.

'It's weird that they didn't know what was wrong with you and now they don't even know what's made you better, but I don't care – all that matters is that you'll be coming home soon,' Kate beamed. 'I can't wait.'

'Your mum's still got to take it easy,' her dad told her. 'If she became ill without warning then it might happen again.'

'No, it won't,' Kate's mum said softly.

'But if you don't know what put you in here, love,' said Kate's dad, 'how can you be so sure?'

'I just know,' Kate's mum replied. 'Anyway, you two will keep your eyes on me, won't you?'

'I'll do whatever you want, Mum,' Kate said.

'Even your homework?' her mum said with a smile.

Kate nodded and laughed.

'I got better because of you, Kate,' her mum told her, touching her cheek. 'You always cheer me up when you visit me. You and your dad.' She leaned forward and kissed Kate. 'Thank you.'

Kate hugged her mum.

'I'm sorry,' her mum whispered, looking a little upset.

'What for?' Kate asked, surprised.

'For all the trouble I've caused. All the worry . . .' her mum replied.

'But everything's going to be fine now, Mum, isn't it?' Kate said.

Her mum smiled but didn't answer.

'What are you thinking about, Kate?' Susie asked at school the following day. 'You've hardly said a word all lunch-time,' she added, pushing another crisp into her mouth. 'Is it your mum?'

Kate shook her head. Staring out across the playground, she bit into her sandwich and chewed thoughtfully. 'I know this is going to sound stupid,' she said, 'but have you ever heard voices?'

'What kind of voices?' Susie asked.

'You know, *voices* – when there doesn't seem to be anyone there.'

Susie looked thoughtful. 'Well, I read in one of my brother's science magazines that alien waves could be picked up by fillings in teeth,' she told Kate.

'Alien waves? What are they?' Kate asked.

'Well, the sounds from flying saucers I suppose, from spaceships. Not sure I believe it myself,'

Susie replied, shrugging. 'Seems a bit far-fetched that aliens can contact people by using their fillings. But it's supposed to be something to do with the metal fillings being a conductor or something – like a radio,' she finished. Then her eyes widened. 'Why? Have *you* been hearing voices, then?'

'Yes . . . well, I don't know. I'm probably imagining it. But I'm sure it wasn't aliens,' Kate said, smiling. 'These were proper voices. People having conversations.'

'It *could* have been aliens,' Susie insisted. 'I mean, they might look just like us, mightn't they? *You* might be one for all I know.'

Kate grinned. 'If people can pick up alien waves with their fillings,' she said, 'do you think your brother could pick up a radio station on his brace?'

Both of them collapsed with laughter.

As she neared the church on her way home, Kate felt tense, wondering whether she'd hear voices again. Or was she really just imagining all this?

'I'll see you about six, then, after you've dropped the kids off.'

'That's right. Twelve red roses, to be delivered to Ms B. Burkeman. Thank you.'

'Don't forget to pick up some dog food on your way home.'

Kate closed her eyes. It had started again. All different voices – seemingly unrelated.

'What time does the film start? We don't want to be late.'

'Tell her I'll wear that black dress. I don't want to turn up in the same outfit as Kelly.'

The voices were raining in on her like missiles.

Feeling panicked now, Kate opened her eyes again, wanting to run, escape from the noise. And then she saw it. A shiny-looking plaque, attached to the church wall near the entrance.

ROOF OF ST BARTOL'S CHURCH
RESTORED BY NATIONAL TELECOM

She looked up. Perched high on the steeple of the church, like a metallic beacon, was a mobile phone antenna.

'Yes, it's lovely, isn't it, the new roof?'

At first Kate thought it was another of the voices in her head. And then she felt a touch on her arm.

'Are you all right, dear?' came the voice.

Kate turned to see a kind-faced old lady staring at her, looking concerned. Kate nodded dumbly, unable to explain what was happening to her.

The old lady smiled and pointed to the roof. 'They paid for it,' she went on. 'They did it in exchange for Reverend Dodds allowing them to put the mobile phone mast-thingy up there, you see.' She studied Kate's features for a moment and shook her head. 'Are you sure you're all right, dear? You look awfully pale.'

Kate nodded again, and then hurried away, her mind reeling. As she did so, the voices began to lessen.

She stepped back towards the church again.

'I'm telling you, they should have had at least two more goals before half-time . . .'

'You have reached the voice mail of National Telecom mobile phone number . . .'

'Oh . . . hello . . . This mobile phone I bought. I'd like to change it.'

That was the answer. It had to be.

Kate wasn't going mad. The voices she'd heard, the snippets of conversation, they were being relayed backwards and forwards on mobile phones.

And somehow, Kate was picking up conversations from the phone mast.

'Mum, you look so much better,' Kate said happily, looking at her mum who was sitting up in bed. She had a couple of pillows propping her up and much of the healthy colour she used to have had returned to her cheeks.

'I *feel* much better, Kate,' her mum told her, sipping

at a cup of tea. 'But how do *you* feel, darling?' she asked Kate.

'I'm fine,' Kate shrugged. For a moment, she wondered whether to mention the voices, but it seemed selfish. Her mum needed all her strength to get better. The last thing she wanted was to be worrying about Kate.

'Are you sure?' her mum persisted. 'Everything all right at school? Susie all right?'

'Mum, I told you. Everything is fine. Why do you keep asking?'

'I'm concerned. You've had a lot of responsibility since I came into hospital. It hasn't been easy for you. I know that. I'm sorry.'

'You keep saying sorry, Mum. It's not your fault you got ill,' Kate said.

Her mum shook her head slowly. 'You know I love you, don't you, Kate?' she said.

'Mu-um,' Kate said, blushing.

'Just remember, I'll always be there for you,' her mum said, quietly.

* * *

'*A taxi at eleven thirty – yes, I've got that.*'

'*Get out of here and don't come back.*'

Kate opened her eyes and turned over in bed so fast that she nearly fell out. *Not again! Not in my house! How is this happening?* she thought desperately. She put her hands to her ears in frustration, wanting the voices to stop. Somehow, she was now picking up mobile phone conversations even when she wasn't close to an antenna.

She stared at the ceiling but it was a long time before she drifted off into an exhausted sleep.

She awoke with a start the following morning. Sitting up in bed, Kate cautiously touched her ears. She yawned – and could hear herself clearly. No mad collection of voices drowned out the sound.

Kate felt a little more at ease as she washed and dressed.

'*Sorry, darling – I'm going to be late – traffic's awful!*'

Kate swallowed hard. *Please don't let it be starting again!* she thought.

'Oh, let's go to the Italian — I really fancy spaghetti tonight . . .'

Kate waited awhile, listening to the snippets of conversation passing through. The babbling inside her head seemed to have settled to a manageable level now. How it got there was another matter, though.

Her dad was finishing his breakfast hurriedly when she wandered into the kitchen, the voices still buzzing inside her head.

Kate wondered about confiding in him.

'I've got to go, sweetheart,' he said, rushing past her. 'Or I'll be late for work.' He stopped, turned back and kissed the top of her head, then disappeared out of the front door. 'Love you!'

'Love you too, Dad,' Kate sighed, listening to the sound of his car starting outside.

She quickly ate a bowl of cornflakes and then set off for school.

Kate approached the church nervously. But now that the phone conversations were reaching her just as easily away from the antenna, nothing much changed as she drew near.

There were several cars parked outside. A funeral was taking place.

Kate could now hear church music mixing with the voices – the congregation was singing "The Old Rugged Cross". She remembered overhearing someone in the church mention that hymn. They'd been talking about the funeral of a lady with an unusual name. What was it again? Augustine something or other. And she'd wanted everyone to wear purple and white.

Kate paused, looking up at the telephone antenna on the church roof, wondering what she should do about the snippets of conversation that still mingled with the mournful hymn inside her head.

The hymn came to an end and Kate saw six men dressed in black emerge from the church carrying a coffin on their shoulders. Each of them wore tall top hats, with purple ribbons wound around them. They fluttered in the breeze like flags of mourning.

The congregation followed – all dressed in purple and white.

As the coffin was turned, she saw that the purple and white flowers adorning the coffin lid formed a name.

AUGUSTINE

Kate didn't wait to see any more. She turned and walked hurriedly down the road. She wanted to cry out. To scream at the voices to get out of her head. She wanted to ignore the even more scary thing that had just become obvious to her: some of the conversations she was hearing hadn't even happened yet! She'd heard Augustine's funeral *days* ago. But it had taken place this morning.

What did Reverend Dodds call it? Kate thought. *Witchcraft? But I'm not a witch!*

The dustmen were making their rounds, emptying bins into the back of their slowly moving dustcart. The noise of the cart's crusher as it chewed up the rubbish was deafening. Louder even than the voices inside Kate's head.

'Kate.'

She kept walking.

'Kate.'

The voice grew louder than the others and Kate realized it was coming not from within her skull but from just behind her.

She turned to see Susie scurrying across the street towards her.

'I thought you were ignoring me,' Susie said, catching her breath.

'I didn't hear you,' Kate told her friend.

'I'm not surprised with the racket the dustmen are making,' Susie replied. 'But I'll tell you someone else who'll be making a racket today: Mrs Lawson.'

'Why?' Kate asked.

'Hello! Because hardly anyone will have got that maths homework she set right. I mean, I know she's a bit of a slave-driver but even *she's* never set us anything that hard before. Please don't tell me you thought it was easy.'

'Oh, Susie. I haven't even looked at it,' Kate said.

'Oops . . .' Susie said. 'Any other teacher would probably let you off, what with your mum being in hospital and that – but not Mrs Lawson.'

Kate sucked in a deep breath. 'What am I going to do?' she murmured.

'Er . . . leave the country? Have plastic surgery so she doesn't recognize you?' Susie suggested. 'Sorry, there's no point copying mine – I know it's wrong, so she's bound to guess one of us has copied if we both have all the same wrong answers.'

'I'll do the homework after registration,' Kate decided.

'It took me two hours to do one little part of it,' said Susie. 'And there's two whole pages of questions to work through. You'll never do that after registration.'

As they entered the playground, Susie went on and on, worrying about the maths homework. 'I mean,' she continued, 'how can she expect us to do all that in two nights? I bet she never got homework like that when she was at school.'

'I'm so sorry, Mr Johns. I really do feel quite unwell . . .'

The voice belonged to Mrs Lawson.

'So as I won't be in class today, I'd appreciate it if you'd tell the class that they can have an extra day to complete the work.'

Kate turned to Susie. 'Maybe Mrs Lawson won't be in today,' she said as the bell went.

'Of course she will,' Susie protested. 'She's never off. She never gets ill. She's like some kind of alien, she never even gets colds.'

Kate looked at Susie and, for a second, considered telling her friend that she'd just picked up Mrs Lawson's telephone call in her head. Then she thought better of it.

She walked over to Daisy Barton. 'Daisy,' she said.

Daisy Barton turned. 'What do you want?' she asked.

'You've done the maths homework, haven't you?' Kate asked.

'Of course I have,' Daisy replied sniffily. 'Why? Haven't you?'

Kate shook her head. 'But listen, I'll do a deal with you. If Mrs Lawson is off sick then Susie and I get to copy your answers, right? If she's not, then you can have my WestZone concert ticket.'

Daisy looked at her in shock, and then a smile crept across her face. 'Deal,' she said. 'You must be really scared of Mrs Lawson, that's all I can say!'

'Kate – what are you doing?' Susie whispered. 'You'd better be right.'

'I will be,' Kate said, confidently.

'And if you're wrong?' Susie whispered worriedly.

'I don't think I will be,' Kate whispered back.

'Well, we'll soon know if you're right,' Susie said. 'Maths is the first lesson.'

After registration and assembly, the class all waited anxiously for Mrs Lawson to arrive.

But the door opened to let in Mr Johns the head teacher, instead. He nodded a greeting. 'I'm sorry to tell you that Mrs Lawson isn't feeling very well today,' he informed them. 'She's just called me on her mobile phone to say she started the journey here, but has now turned around to go back home and won't be coming in.'

Someone at the back of the class cheered.

Daisy's jaw dropped, her lips opening and closing like a goldfish.

Kate let out a sigh that was a mixture of relief and delight and glanced sideways at Susie who shrugged and mouthed silently at her, 'How did you know?'

'Mrs Lawson told me that she set you all some homework,' Mr Johns continued. 'And she asked me to tell you that you can have this lesson and until she returns to complete it.'

There was another cheer.

Kate looked at Susie again and smiled.

Susie leaned close to her. 'You must be a witch,' she whispered, grinning broadly.

At first Kate thought that she was dreaming.

Then she realized that the words and hysterical voices whirling around inside her head were all too real.

She sucked in a deep breath and tried to focus on what the voices were saying. It was almost like trying to tune in a radio.

'Leaving the band . . . can't believe it . . .'

The words continued to spin through her head.

'. . . millions of records . . . sell-out tour . . . WestZone won't be the same without him . . .'

Kate closed her eyes tightly again for a moment and one single sentence seemed to glow inside her mind like torchlight in the dark.

'Nooo! How can Richie do this to us?'

Kate shook her head slightly. Richie – leaving WestZone? That was *worse* than a nightmare. He was her favourite singer in the world.

She looked across to her bedside table where her ticket for WestZone's sell-out show was lying there like a trophy.

Swinging herself out of bed, Kate crossed the landing quietly, wincing when one of the floorboards creaked. She waited to see if she'd woken her dad but then, deciding she hadn't, she continued on down the stairs and into the living-room and flicked on the light.

The daily paper was lying on the sofa. Kate flicked through it quickly.

No mention of Richie leaving the band in there – and surely, Kate reasoned, one of her friends would have mentioned it, would have heard about it by now. Especially Susie. She was mad on WestZone – though her favourite band member was Karl. You couldn't see her wallpaper for posters of him.

Kate waited a moment then switched on the TV, hurriedly turning down the volume.

The news came and went with no mention of Richie leaving. She tried Teletext and Ceefax.

Nothing.

She turned off the TV and curled up on the sofa, her heart beating fast. It was clear that Richie hadn't left the band. Not yet.

She thought about the telephone conversation she'd heard taking place at a funeral – when it hadn't even happened yet. And how she'd heard Mrs Lawson's call to Mr Johns before that had happened too.

If the voices in her head were correct again, then Richie leaving WestZone was still to come.

Kate sat still for a long time before heading back to bed. But it was ages before she could sleep. And not just because of the voices buzzing inside her brain.

When the alarm woke Kate the next morning she still felt a little groggy from lack of sleep, but as she looked across at her WestZone ticket, an idea began to form in her mind.

She put the ticket into the side pocket of her schoolbag then hurried downstairs.

Kate ate her breakfast quickly that morning and she was out of the door before her dad, who just about managed to say goodbye to her before she hurried off down the road.

'Why have you got your WestZone ticket with you?' Susie wanted to know when Kate took it out of her bag at school. 'You'd better hide it from Daisy Barton, she'll only start moaning again because she was too late to buy one herself.'

'Well, she can buy this one if she wants to,' Kate told her.

'What?' said Susie, open-mouthed. 'I thought you were desperate to see Richie live. I read that WestZone won't be touring again for at least a year.'

'Well, if Daisy wants this one she can buy it,' Kate replied. 'I've gone off WestZone a bit, and now I'd rather buy my mum a nice present for when she comes out of hospital.'

'Ah, that's really kind – but I can't wait to see Karl in the flesh!' Susie smiled. 'I wouldn't sell for a million pounds!'

Kate grinned.

'Well, all right then . . . maybe for a million pounds,' chuckled Susie.

They saw Daisy Barton walking across the playground with her mates.

Kate strode straight across to her, the ticket proudly displayed. 'You wanted a ticket for the WestZone gig, didn't you, Daisy?' she asked.

Daisy's eyes widened as she saw the ticket. 'Is this a joke?' she asked suspiciously. 'Trying to make me jealous?'

Kate shook her head. 'If you want it you can buy it off me,' she told her. 'I've not as keen on WestZone as I was.'

'All right,' Daisy said. 'I'll go home at lunch-time and get the money.'

'Sounds good to me,' Kate smiled.

Daisy grabbed her arm. 'You'd better not change your mind.'

'I won't – I promise,' Kate said.

'Cool,' Daisy grinned. She and her friends walked off.

'That was easy, wasn't it?' Kate said, looking down at her ticket.

Susie stared at Kate and shook her head. 'I still don't know how you could have done it though,

Kate. There's no way I'm selling mine. I'd go mad if I had to miss WestZone.'

'I think I'll survive,' Kate replied as they walked to their classroom. The voices in her head had stilled to a low buzz. A little like flies around a light. It was annoying but she could put up with it. And by the time she'd collected her money from Daisy that afternoon, her head was pretty clear.

'You could get three or four CDs with that,' Susie said enviously. 'Or a couple of new tops.'

Kate pushed the money into her purse. 'I told you, I want to get something for my mum as a coming home present,' she said, looking out of the window.

'Do you know when she might be leaving the hospital?' Susie asked.

'Not yet, but soon I hope,' Kate replied. 'It'll be great to have her home again.'

When Kate arrived home from school, she made herself a sandwich and then wandered into the living-room and put the TV on. She switched to one of her favourite music shows.

Kate immediately noticed that there were photos of WestZone behind the presenter. She reached for the remote and turned up the sound.

'So, the unthinkable has happened . . .' the presenter said. 'In the last hour, Richie has announced he has left WestZone! Hard to believe, I know. He is due to appear shortly at a press conference to talk of his future plans . . .'

Kate chewed thoughtfully on her sandwich as she watched.

'WestZone has sold over twenty million albums worldwide, with Richie as lead singer,' the presenter continued. 'The band has said that the forthcoming tour will go ahead – but unfortunately for those Richie fans out there, without him.'

The phone rang.

Kate got to her feet and picked it up. 'Hello,' she said, one eye still on the TV screen.

She recognized the voice at the other end of the

line immediately. It was Daisy Barton.

'Kate, I've just heard about Richie leaving WestZone,' Daisy told her.

'I know, I just saw it on the TV,' Kate replied.

'Well, the only reason I wanted to see them was because I like Richie!' Daisy yelled down the phone. 'I don't want to go any more – I want my money back!'

'Sorry, Daisy,' Kate said firmly. 'It's nothing to do with me that you don't want to go to the concert any more.'

Kate hung up and then walked back to the sofa and sat down, gazing at the TV screen. The presenter was still going on about WestZone.

Kate took another bite of her sandwich and wondered how Daisy Barton was feeling.

'Listen, I'm not going to put up with much more of this. My heating's been off for two days now and no one's come to fix it.'

A man's voice. He was angry.

'Did you see the state of her in that dress the other night? I

told *Zena that I wouldn't be caught dead in something like that.'*

A woman's voice this time.

Kate heard the snippets of conversation moving around inside her head. She felt tired and the low buzzing of the voices was making her feel even more sleepy. She hadn't slept well for the last two nights and now, seated close to the soothing warmth of the radiator in the classroom, she was having trouble staying awake.

'I know it's sad about her dog dying. She'd had it for ten years. It was like a member of the family, I suppose.'

Another woman's voice.

'So, in the Greek myths, most of the characters were either punished or rewarded by the gods. A bit like Kate is likely to be punished by me for not listening in class.'

Immediately, Kate jerked her head up from her desk, to see the face of the teacher staring at her.

'Sorry, Mr Currell,' Kate said.

'Is the story of Cassandra boring you, Kate?' Mr Currell asked.

Several of her classmates were laughing now. Kate felt herself blushing. 'No, Mr Currell,' she said.

'So, Cassandra was given the gift of prophecy by Zeus, king of the gods,' Mr Currell continued. 'She was able to see into the future, but the problem was, no one would believe her prophecies, and more tragically, she was powerless to change what was going to happen.'

Kate looked apologetically at Mr Currell and tried to concentrate on the words she heard coming from the front of the class.

'Matt really fancies her. I asked him.'

Kate shook her head, trying to ignore the new voice.

'He fancies Kate. I'm telling you the truth. I spoke to him after he played football yesterday.'

Suddenly Kate didn't want the voice to go away. Matt fancies Kate? It could only be Matt Albert. Not

47

only was he the best footballer in the school, he was also the fittest boy by a mile.

Matt fancies Kate.

'Wow,' Kate said loudly.

'Something interesting, Kate?' Mr Currell asked her pointedly. 'Have you found a part of Cassandra's story that's finally grabbed your attention?'

'Sorry, Mr Currell,' Kate replied, her cheeks turning red.

She dropped her head towards the textbook opened on her desk, as much to mask her delight as anything else. So Matt Albert fancied her, did he? Well, perhaps it was about time she told him that she felt the same. Wow – she might have her first boyfriend!

Kate glanced at the clock and saw that it was almost lunch-time. She decided she'd go and speak to Matt then. He was always to be found in the same place: kicking a ball around with his mates on the school field – usually with three or four girls watching him as they pretended to talk about something else.

The time passed slowly for Kate, but when the bell finally sounded she was the first one out of the classroom.

Kate ate her lunch hurriedly, impatient to get over to the playing-field and wait for an opportunity to talk to Matt.

As she got up to leave, Susie got up too. 'Where are you rushing off to?' she asked curiously.

'I need to do something,' Kate told her. 'I'll tell you all about it later – won't be long.' Then she hurried away, leaving Susie looking puzzled.

Kate forced her way down the crowded school corridor until she reached the exit into the playground. She could see that there was already a group of boys from the next year up, kicking a ball about. As she drew closer, she picked out Matt Albert among them.

Matt fancies Kate. She felt a tingle run up her spine.

But the thought of marching across the field in

front of all his friends and saying that she fancied him too, was way too embarrassing. Kate decided she'd watch him and his mates playing football, and then try to get to talk to him on his own, afterwards.

Two of the boys kicking the ball around had already noticed Kate standing there. She smiled at them. Maybe they already knew that their mate Matt fancied her.

'Who did you say Matt fancied?'

Kate winced, the boy's voice in her ear was so loud. There was a crackling sound like static.

'Kate. But I don't think she knows yet.'

Kate recognized the same whispered voice in her head she'd heard in class. She smiled to herself.

'Kate's in the year above him, though. I suppose he likes the fact that she's so sporty. And she does look great in her netball outfit.'

For a second, Kate was confused. And then she remembered tall, slim, sporty, netball-playing, blonde Kate Kirby in the year above them.

Was *that* who Matt fancied? Not her? Kate went all hot and cold in embarrassment.

'Fancy a game, Kate?' one of the boys called, kicking the ball towards her.

Matt Albert ran past her after the ball. He didn't even look at her.

Kate felt her face burning red. 'I was looking for Susie, I thought I saw her come this way,' she lied. And she turned and headed back towards the playground.

'If you want to play, just come back and tell us,' one of the other boys shouted.

She heard laughter echoing behind her. But the laughter was nothing compared to the embarrassment she would have felt if she'd gone through with talking to Matt. What a narrow escape! Kate felt almost sick at the thought of how close she had come to making an absolute fool of herself.

The voices had their uses, but it seemed that they could get her into trouble too, if she wasn't careful!

* * *

'That noise is enough to drive anyone mad,' said Susie as she and Kate approached school the following day.

There was a lorry parked in the road outside the tower block that loomed over the school. Part of the street had been dug up; the eardrum-shattering sound of a road drill filled the air.

Kate didn't answer. The loud and abrasive sound of nearby construction meant that she was spared the more intrusive sounds of voices inside her head for a while. She saw two men unloading a large black metal object from the back of the lorry.

She realized with horror that it was a mobile phone mast, identical to the one on top of the church spire. 'They're putting that on top of the flats?' she gasped in alarm.

'Yes, didn't you hear about it on the local news?' Susie asked. 'They're putting them up all over town. Some of the residents are really angry about it.'

Kate winced. She'd had a headache from all the snippets of phone conversations coming into her head since she'd woken up that morning. Over the last few days there had been more and more of them. And no wonder, if mobile phone masts were being put up all over town. But now there was going to be one next to school too. It would be intolerable!

'Are you all right, Kate?' Susie asked.

Kate shrugged vaguely, her gaze fixed on the top of the tower block. 'I've got a bad headache, that's all . . .' she said. As they watched, Kate saw the mast being raised – a black arrow-head against the clouds.

During the history lesson that morning, the hum of voices coming into Kate's head suddenly escalated to a roar, rushing in at her from all directions. The new mast must have started to work. It felt to Kate as if her brain was a roundabout in the centre of a busy junction, words driving at it from everywhere at once. She put a hand to the back of her neck.

'You should see the school nurse if you don't feel any better,' Susie whispered.

Kate tried to nod but the pain was too intense. She feared she would either pass out or simply go crazy right there on the spot.

'You'll have to go to the nurse,' Susie insisted.

'You're right,' Kate agreed. She didn't really want to go to see Nurse Williams. The rather sour-faced school nurse was never very sympathetic. But Kate had to do *something*.

She put her hand up to ask their teacher's permission.

Slowly, trying to keep her head as still as possible, Kate approached Nurse Williams's office. She knocked on the outer door and then walked in.

From the small waiting area, Kate could see Nurse Williams at her desk in the office beyond. She was on the phone. She signalled for Kate to take a seat.

Kate slumped on to the chair and put her hands to her head again. The pain was increasing.

'Hang on a minute,' Nurse Williams said. 'I've got someone waiting. I'll just see what they want.' She put the phone to one side and came out to Kate, eyeing her somewhat suspiciously. 'Yes, dear?' she said.

'I've got a really bad headache,' Kate told her. 'I was wondering if there was something you could give me for it.'

The nurse looked at her again then nodded. 'Wait there,' she said, and then disappeared back into her office.

Kate saw her pick the phone up again.

'Another one with a headache,' Nurse Williams said into the mouthpiece. 'Backache. Stomachache. Headache. They use any excuse to get out of lessons, some of them.'

Kate felt like calling over that she *wasn't* using the pain as an excuse. She would have given anything to make it stop. Just as she would have given anything to silence the ever-chattering voices inside her head.

'Always complaining,' Nurse Williams continued to her unseen friend. 'I'm fed up with it. They're all the same. Anything to get off school for a couple of hours.'

She returned with two white tablets and a glass of water. 'Take these,' she said, sharply. 'And then you can return straight back to class.'

'But I think it might be a migraine,' Kate replied, accepting the tablets. 'I feel a bit sick and dizzy too.'

Nurse Williams rolled her eyes. 'So you want to go home, do you?'

'Yes, please,' Kate said faintly. 'I don't think I could go through the rest of the afternoon like this.'

Nurse Williams sighed and called Kate's dad.

He arrived within half an hour.

Kate climbed gratefully into his waiting car and lay back in the passenger seat.

'You look awful, Kate,' her dad said worriedly, reaching out to touch her forehead. 'Let's get you home. It's a bit of luck I'm on the late shift at the factory tonight, otherwise I wouldn't have been there when the nurse rang.'

'I just need to lie down, Dad, and try to get rid of this headache,' Kate told him.

'I hope you can sleep with all the noise,' her dad said.

'What noise?' Kate asked.

'Outside the house. National Telecom are putting up one of those mobile phone antennae right across the street.'

Kate almost burst into tears. *Not another one*, she thought.

As her dad swung the car into their street she saw the National Telecom van parked across the road and the men busily erecting the antenna.

Kate practically fell from the car and her dad hurried around to the passenger side to help her.

'Come on, let's get you inside,' he said comfortingly.

Kate's vision swam, and she thought her legs were going to buckle. Her dad supported her as they made their way into the house. The sound from outside dimmed but the roaring inside Kate's head continued.

Her dad helped her into the living-room and she sat down on the sofa.

He knelt beside her, stroking her forehead. 'Trust you to feel bad today of all days,' he said, smiling, still gently brushing her hair from her face. 'I wanted to give you the good news when you got home.'

'What good news?' she asked groggily.

'I spoke to the doctor at the hospital today and he said that your mum can come home in a couple of days. Whatever was wrong with her has now almost completely cleared up. She still needs time to get back to normal but she's improving all the time.'

Kate gave a weak smile. 'Mum starts getting better and I start to feel bad,' she joked.

'I spoke to your mum myself on the phone,' her dad continued. 'It was great to hear her sounding more like her old self. She said she couldn't wait to speak to you. There's something she wants to tell you.' He got up. 'I'll go and make us a cup of tea, eh?

You just lie here and try and get some rest. We'll go and see your mum tonight before I go to work.'

Suddenly Kate felt she just couldn't wait any longer to see her mum again. 'No, Dad, I want to see her now,' she said, sitting up. She winced at the pain inside her head.

'But you're not well enough, Kate,' her dad said, looking concerned.

'I want to see her, Dad. Please . . .' Kate pleaded. 'I really miss her when I'm not feeling well.' She hesitated. 'Dad, I haven't been feeling well for a while now,' she confessed. 'But I haven't wanted to worry Mum, her being ill herself. Now though . . . Well, I just want to talk to her about it all . . .'

Her dad looked at her then reached out gently and touched her forehead with his hand.

'I understand, Kate, and it's good of you to consider your mum.'

'So can we go and see her now, Dad?'

'Come on, then,' he smiled. 'I'll get my coat.'

* * *

59

Kate's mum was sitting up, the bandages removed from her throat, her hair done, and her make-up on. She looked like her old self. Healthy and beaming. 'Hello, darling,' she said to Kate in a clear, if somewhat husky, voice.

Kate rushed over to her mum and hugged her.

'I didn't expect you at this time of the day,' said her mum. 'You should be at school.'

'I had to go home,' Kate told her. 'I had a terrible headache. I've been getting them for days now. Headaches and—'

Kate's mum placed a hand on one of Kate's. 'I bet you haven't been drinking enough, darling,' she said, interrupting. She looked at Kate's dad. 'Would you mind going and getting a couple of drinks from the machine, Harry?' she asked.

'Of course,' Kate's dad replied with a smile. 'Won't be long.'

When he had gone, Kate's mum turned and gazed at Kate intently. 'And what else has been happening to you, Kate?' she asked quietly.

'Phone conversations. Coming into my head. I can hear people talking, Mum,' Kate told her. 'On mobile phones. All the time. And sometimes, the stuff I hear hasn't even happened yet. It's like I hear what's going to happen before it actually does. Like I can hear the future. But I know that's stupid. What's happening to me, Mum? Am I going crazy?'

'No, Kate, you're not . . .' Her mum lowered her gaze slightly and squeezed Kate's hand. 'Kate . . .' she continued hesitantly, 'I knew this time would come for you and now that it has, you need to know what's happening.'

Kate looked warily at her mum.

'You have a gift, Kate,' her mum told her. 'At least that's what we call it. Some people might call it a curse but it can be used for good so we've always looked on it as a good thing.'

'Mum, I don't understand,' Kate said, feeling a little scared now.

Kate's mum sighed. 'It started with your great-great-grandmother, Elizabeth,' she began. 'Elizabeth was celebrating her twelfth birthday. The house where her family lived was right next to a telegraph pole. There was a terrible storm raging, but Elizabeth insisted on trying out her new umbrella. She went out into the garden, and in a freak accident, lightning hit the pole and then forked into Elizabeth.' Kate's mum paused for a moment, as if waiting to be sure that Kate was taking the information in.

'At first, everyone thought Elizabeth was dead,' she continued. 'But somehow, she had survived. And she had also contracted the gift.'

'What *is* the gift, Mum?' Kate asked her impatiently.

'As Elizabeth got older she developed the ability to overhear telephone conversations – just like you can now,' Kate's mum explained. 'And when her own daughter turned twelve, it was passed on to her too. It's been passed on from generation to generation ever since – always from mother to daughter, when the daughter turned twelve. And from the time you were born I knew that you'd have to inherit it one day.'

Then she sighed. 'But by the time you turned twelve, three months ago, the world had become so filled with telephones, the voices had become almost unbearable. I decided not to inflict the gift on you. I resisted and resisted the urge . . .'

Her eyes filled with tears. 'Kate, I think that if I hadn't given in and passed the gift on to you when I did, I would have died . . .'

Kate's eyes widened. '*That* is what made you ill?' she asked incredulously.

Her mum nodded. 'But I couldn't tell anyone. Elizabeth confided in two people and they both collapsed and died.'

Kate shook her head, finding it hard to take all this in. 'So that's why you began to get better again? Because you passed the gift on to me?' she asked.

Her mum nodded again. 'When I kissed your ear . . .' She wiped away a tear that ran down her cheek. 'Do you remember? Just before I asked you to buy flowers for Gran's grave.'

Kate nodded, and then hugged her mum. 'It's not your fault, Mum.'

Kate's mum gave her a watery smile. 'Thanks, darling – I was worried that you'd hate me . . .' She blew her nose. 'But you must learn how to control it. You have to master the gift, not let it take over your mind. I can help you do that. Gran knew how dangerous it could be if it was used wrongly. She warned me about it just like I'm warning you now. She was frightened of it towards the end. She heard of her own death . . .'

'What do you mean?' Kate asked, startled.

Kate's mum squeezed her hand again. 'She heard her doctor talking on his phone with the hospital. She knew what was going to happen but she couldn't stop it . . . That's why your gran and I moved home so many times. We had to.'

'I don't understand,' Kate said.

'People are always scared by what they don't

understand, darling,' Kate's mum said sadly. 'Sometimes your gran tried to warn someone of something that was about to happen – but it would scare them. Gran was once even called a witch, and they threatened to burn our house down if we didn't leave.'

'And I first heard voices in a churchyard where people had been victimized for being thought witches too,' Kate said flatly, as she remembered the scratched-out gravestones Reverend Dodds had talked to her about.

'As I said, Kate, people are afraid of things they don't understand. I want you to understand. I want you to let me help you cope with the gift – and use it to help others, even if we must guard against letting them know what we are doing, to protect ourselves.'

Kate sat still on the edge of her mum's bed, her head bowed, voices whirling around inside her brain. '*Am* I a witch?' she asked quietly.

Her mum pulled her close and hugged her. 'No.

You're not a witch,' she smiled. 'You're not a freak and you're not a monster. You're just . . . special.'

'But what if I don't want to be?' Kate asked, her irritation rising. She felt tears stinging her own eyes now.

'Don't be angry, Kate,' her mum pleaded. 'It won't do any good.'

'Tea for everyone,' Kate's dad said, walking in balancing three plastic beakers of tea.

'I just want to go home,' Kate said. 'Take me home, Dad, please.'

Her dad looked surprised. He looked at Kate then at her mum. 'I thought we were going to have a drink,' he said.

'I'd like to go now, please,' Kate insisted. She looked at her mum. 'Unless there's anything else Mum wants to tell me.' Then she turned and walked away.

'We'll talk more when I get home, Kate,' her mum called. 'Everything'll be fine.'

Kate wished she could believe that.

* * *

It was after midnight. Kate knew that. But how late she had no idea. She didn't bother looking at her watch. All she knew was that she couldn't sleep. The voices were still inside her head but so too was the news her mum had given her earlier that evening: the knowledge of why the voices were there and the fact that, as far as Kate knew, they would be there for the rest of her life.

She turned over in an effort to get to sleep but it was useless.

Her mum's words, the words of other conversations from inside her brain, they all mingled together to form one mass of confusion.

Then suddenly a conversation came into her head with such crystal clarity it was as if it was being spoken directly into her ear.

'You'd better be right about this job. I'm not getting caught again. Ten months in prison was enough for me. If anyone gets in the way this time, they'll be sorry.'

This voice was low and menacing. Little more

than a growl. Kate felt a shiver run down her spine.

'It'll be fine. Trust me. The owners are away for the weekend, the whole family. There's no burglar alarm. We'll be able to break in really easily. He keeps his collection of gold coins in a cupboard in the dining-room. It'll be a piece of cake.'

This voice was quiet and nervous.

Kate sat up. Susie's dad had a collection of gold coins. And she and her family were away for the weekend. Then she shook her head. It must be a coincidence, surely.

The low, menacing voice cut in again: *'Just remember: this job is too big to mess up. If there is anyone inside the house when we go in, then we finish them — nice and clean. Tell me the address again.'*

'Twenty-two Acacia Avenue . . .'

There was a deafening hiss of static in Kate's ear and she winced. Her heart was thumping. That was Susie's house! It was going to be robbed!

She waited, hoping to hear more of the conversation, but there was nothing. Instead she picked up two people talking about a movie they'd just watched. She let out a breath of frustration.

What should she do now? Alone in the darkness, Kate realized that she might be able to stop the robbery. Was this what her mum had meant about the gift being used for good?

She would have to go to the police. She would warn them. They'd be waiting for the criminals; they'd catch them in the act.

Kate nodded to herself. She even managed a smile.

She switched on her bedside light and fumbled for a paper and pencil, writing down as much of the conversation as she could remember.

She'd ring the police and tell them what she knew. Tell them she'd heard a robbery being planned. She didn't have to tell them how she knew. She didn't even have to give them her name. For the first time in what seemed like ages, Kate felt in control.

She crept downstairs and dialled the number of the local police station.

'Hello, police,' a voice said. 'Can I help you?'

'I want to report a robbery,' Kate said.

'Where?' the policeman asked.

'At number 22 Acacia Avenue.'

'And when did it happen?'

Kate swallowed hard. 'Well, it hasn't happened yet. But it is *going* to be robbed.'

'Oh, really, when?' the policeman asked.

'Well . . . I don't actually know,' Kate replied. 'But I've just heard two men talking about it.'

'And where did you hear them talking about it?' the policeman asked.

'I was in my bedroom,' Kate told him.

There was a pause.

'In your bedroom?' the policeman asked. 'The men were in your bedroom?'

'No,' Kate replied impatiently. 'I heard their telephone conversation – in my head.'

Kate heard a sound somewhere between a cough and a groan at the other end of the line.

'Inside your head?' the policeman said, slowly.

'And where are these men coming from to rob the house at 22 Acacia Avenue? Mars? Saturn? Jupiter?'

'I did hear them, honestly!' Kate insisted. 'They're going to steal a collection of gold coins!'

The policeman sighed. 'So they're going to rob this house, are they? You heard them say so inside your head. You just don't know when they're going to do it?'

'No, I'm sorry, I don't. It could be any time,' Kate agreed. 'And they said if anyone got in their way they would kill them!'

'What is your name, miss?' the policeman asked, sounding more serious now.

Kate hesitated. 'I don't want to give my name,' she said. 'But you've got to believe me.'

'You don't want to give your name because you know you'd be in trouble for making this sort of a call,' the policeman said. 'Now what is your name?'

'This is going to happen, honestly,' Kate said. 'You have to believe me!'

'Well, when it does, you come and let me know. Until then – stop wasting police time.'

Kate slammed down the phone in frustration.

She considered calling Susie on her mobile to tell her about the conversation she'd overheard, but thought better of it. Susie wouldn't be any more likely to believe the story than the policeman, and Kate wouldn't have blamed her.

Kate hurried back upstairs to her bedroom and got dressed. Then she searched out her camera. She checked to see if the camera had a film in it then stuffed it into the pocket of her jacket.

If she could get some photos of the robbers then she could at least show those to the police. They'd have to believe her then.

She went back downstairs and then stepped outside into the cold night and set off in the direction of Susie's house.

It took Kate less than twenty minutes to reach Susie's road. She looked up at the high bushes that formed a natural barrier and shielded the house from prying eyes.

Susie's family home was large with a big front garden and a driveway that ran for about fifty metres from the road to the front of the double garage beside the house.

There were a number of trees around the front of the house and Kate thought that one of those might give her the best vantage point to watch from.

She climbed up into the lower branches of one near to the front door, then took the camera from her pocket and peered through the viewfinder. She had a good shot of the driveway and the front door and windows.

Now, all she had to do was wait.

Inside her head, the voices babbled away without stopping.

'Why won't you just shut up?' Kate muttered, banging her forehead with one hand.

Suddenly she heard two unpleasantly familiar voices inside her head.

'Have you found the girl?'

It was the rasping, gravelly-voiced burglar.

'Yes. Got her.'

The other burglar sounded more edgy and nervous than ever.

'Good. Now finish her – nice and clean.'

Kate swayed in shock, her heart beating madly against her ribs. Were they talking about Susie? Had Susie and her family returned home early? Was Susie going to disturb the robbers? Kate had to stop it happening somehow! But she knew there was no point in calling the police again. If they hadn't believed her the first time they wouldn't believe her now either.

'Do as I say.'

And then something amazing happened. It was as if a switch had been thrown inside Kate's brain. For the first time since the voices had started in the churchyard, there was complete and utter silence inside her mind. Beautiful, undisturbed peace. Like it used to be.

She waited a moment, expecting the voices to begin again, but they didn't.

For a moment she forgot everything except the blissful silence inside her head. Perhaps, as her mum had said, she was at last beginning to gain control of her power.

It was getting colder, and Kate's breath clouded in the air every time she exhaled. She was shivering, despite her thick coat and jumper.

She was about to look at her watch when she heard footsteps coming up the driveway.

It was two men, keeping to the shadows as they drew nearer to the house.

Kate could see that one of them was carrying something in his hand that looked heavy. She thought it might be a metal bar.

She reached into her pocket and pulled out the camera, preparing herself.

The men made straight for a side door. They were inside the house within seconds.

Kate slid from her perch, landing on the ground, and ran across to hide behind some bushes near the side door. From that position, she could get a clear shot of the men as they came out carrying their stolen goods.

She waited.

And waited.

It seemed as if hours passed but no one came back out of the house. Kate felt her heart thumping harder. What if they'd gone out another way and she'd missed them? She'd have no evidence of the robbery to show the police.

Kate decided to go in.

Just inside the doorway was an open trapdoor. Kate looked down the steep flight of stone steps that led to the cellar.

Perhaps it wasn't such a good idea going down there. But she overcame her fear and edged slowly downwards, step by step.

After all – if her best friend was in trouble, she might be the only person who could save her. Mercifully, the voices were still silent in Kate's head, making it easier to listen for any movement.

Even though she knew the dangers of her

situation, Kate couldn't help taking a moment to stare in amazement at the contents of Susie's dad's cellar. It was a gigantic room that ran the length of the entire house, disappearing into black shadows in all directions. There were packing-cases everywhere, some of them open. But there was no sign of the men. Kate went back up the stairs and out into the cold night once more. *The men must have left through the front of the house*, she thought.

And then she spotted the two men making their way back down the driveway.

Kate ducked back behind some bushes and raised her camera, preparing to take some pictures – but she lost her balance and the camera dropped to the ground.

The noise shot through the air like a bullet.

The men turned round and saw Kate.

'Catch her!' the gravelly-voiced robber roared.

Kate had no choice. She knew her only hope was to run back down into the cellar. If she could find somewhere to hide down there then she might escape them. She scrambled into the first open packing-case, pulled the lid shut and lay still, heart pounding, among some wood shavings and polystyrene packaging.

The sound of footsteps came thumping down the steps into the cellar.

She heard the footsteps coming closer. They paused right next to where she was. She heard the dialling of numbers, and the breath of the man as he answered the phone.

Kate could just make out the words coming through the phone. 'You found her yet?' said the voice.

'No,' the man replied, leaning slightly against the case that Kate was hiding in. She squeezed her eyes closed in terror, and hugged her knees. 'Anyone around up there?' he said down the phone.

'Not a soul,' the tinny voice replied. 'Take your time, but make sure you find her.'

It was at that moment that Kate realized with horror that the wood shavings used as packaging inside the case were tickling her nose.

She was going to sneeze.

Kate pinched her nostrils together, desperate to avoid the sneeze that would give her away. She sucked in her breath, and held it, until she could feel pressure behind her eyes and in her head. With a feeling of incredible relief, she felt the sensation pass. Then heard the footsteps move away slightly.

But the footsteps came back.

The lid of the packing-case was lifted.

Kate could hear the voice, tinny and distant from the man's mobile phone.

'Have you found the girl?'

A shadowed face stared down at Kate, the green LCD screen illuminating a rough and stubbly cheek. 'Yes. Got her,' said the other robber.

'Good. Now finish her – nice and clean,' he said.

The other man hesitated.

'Do as I say.'

And then, as when Kate had heard this conversation before, the voices stopped.

Everything went quiet.

A PERFECT FIT

Justin Vafadari brought the ball under control with a single deft touch of his right foot. 'That's a superb first touch from Vafadari!' he called in his best commentator's voice. 'He shapes to go one way then—'

Justin moved the ball effortlessly with the outside of his foot, avoiding a lunging tackle from one of his friends. 'He's away from the clumsy defender!' Justin shouted triumphantly, as his friend went sprawling behind him. 'Just the keeper to beat now. Will he go left or right? The keeper doesn't know what to do.'

Justin shaped to strike the ball hard then leaned back slightly and jabbed his toe under it. The chip was inch perfect. The ball floated over the prone goalkeeper – who had gone to ground expecting a low shot – and into the corner of the net. Justin punched the air with delight. 'Six nil!' he shouted, beaming. 'And the crowd are on their feet to cheer this incredible new talent. Forget Michael Owen. Forget Wayne Rooney. Forget Steven Gerrard or Thierry Henry! The crowd are chanting the name of Justin Vafadari as he completes his double hat trick.'

He glanced at his best friend, Mark Wells, and grinned. 'It *is* six, isn't it?'

'You should know, you've scored them all,' laughed Mark.

Justin and his friends always celebrated the end of the school week with a kickabout in the local park. Once more, Justin controlled the ball effortlessly, rode a clumsy challenge from his friend Paul and played a perfect pass into Mark's path. The goalkeeper never stood a chance. The ball flew past him like a rocket, and Justin and Mark wheeled away in delight. Justin had never played this well in his life. Every touch was brilliant, every pass beautifully weighted. Every shot was of incredible power or delicate brilliance. Even his speed seemed to have increased.

'I think it's those new trainers of yours, making you play better,' said Mark, slapping Justin on the back. 'I wish I had a pair.'

Justin smiled and looked down at his feet. Not only did his new trainers look great, they were also a perfect fit.

Darkness was falling as Justin and Mark said goodbye to the other lads and made their way home.

'Twelve goals in one game,' Mark grinned.

'That's got to be some kind of record.'

Justin was about to answer when the sudden wail of sirens made them both look around.

A fire engine shot past like a huge red bullet, its blue lights spinning. It was followed seconds later by another, both hurtling up the main road and racing round the corner.

'It must be a pretty big fire,' Justin murmured, watching the fire engines speed down the busy road.

'It looks like they're heading for the shopping centre,' added Mark, gazing after the accelerating vehicles.

'Ah, well, nothing to do with us, is it?' Justin said.

As Justin reached his house, he glanced at the front garden and smiled. From the look of it, his mum had been gardening all day. Behind the low and perfectly tended privet hedge, a paved path wound across the lawn to the front door. Around its snakelike curves were flower-beds, each one now weed free and stocked with new shrubs and plants. The assorted colours of their blooms were radiant even in the fading light.

Justin walked up the path towards the front door, shaking his head. All that beautiful lawn that he could have played football on – wasted on flowers and shrubs. Although, if Justin was honest with himself, he enjoyed having a home with a nice colourful garden. Not that he'd ever have told his mates. He could imagine their reaction. *Justin likes flowers – what a girl!* He grinned and shook his head again. No, it would be too much to take.

For as long as Justin could remember, his mum had taken great pride in her flower-beds – she loved how they made their house stand out from most of the others in the street. And for years now, Justin had been doing something he knew would send his mum into a rage if she ever found out about it.

Flower-bed jumping.

It was like a hobby to him. He'd begun with the smaller beds, and graduated to leaping over the larger ones as he'd grown older and bigger. So far, though, clearance of the largest bed, just in front of the living-room window, had eluded him.

Justin had nearly made it so many times, but no matter how he varied his run-up, or at what point he started his jump, the result seemed to be the same. His feet would catch the back of the flower-bed, trampling the borders that his mum spent so long trimming.

He glanced at the house and then stepped on to the lawn and walked across to one end of the biggest bed. He stood there, glancing at its radiant array of flowers.

Just one more jump.

He braced himself ready, and then hesitated.

No – he couldn't. One misjudgement and he'd wreck all the newly planted flowers. Mum would go completely berserk. And besides, if he landed in the mud, he would dirty his new trainers and he didn't want that. No. The next jump could wait until another time.

'Justin!'

The sound of his name caused him to spin round.

His mum was at the living-room window. 'Justin,' she repeated, waving him inside. 'Come on – quick.'

He hurried in, kicking off his new trainers and leaving them in the hall, and then wandered into the living-room.

His mum was staring at the television. 'What is it, Mum?' he asked, slumping into the nearest armchair and gazing at the news report on TV.

'You know that place where you got your new trainers?' his mum asked.

'Where I was *awarded* with my new trainers, Mum,' Justin corrected her, 'for being SportCity's ten thousandth customer, remember?'

'Well, you're lucky you got them when you did,' his mum told him. 'Look.'

Justin moved to the edge of his seat, listening to the reporter's commentary as the TV cameras showed the burned-out shell of the large sports store in town.

'*The fire, which has destroyed much of the building, is believed to have begun in the early hours of the morning,*' the reporter said. '*Police and firemen on the scene have so far been unable to find the cause of the blaze, but arson has not yet been ruled out.*'

'I hope no one was hurt,' said Justin's mum.

'*SportCity is one of the biggest independent sporting goods sellers in the country. So far, no casualties have been confirmed at the shop where the blaze occurred, but two security guards employed there are still missing,*' the TV reporter finished.

'That's really bad,' Justin said.

'Yes, it is,' his mum agreed. 'Still – nothing we can do. The police and firemen are dealing with it.'

'Is dinner ready?' he asked, rubbing his stomach hungrily.

His mum nodded. 'I'll come and dish up,' she said, taking one last glance at the television. 'You're not going round Mark's tonight, are you?'

'No. I'm going to my room to listen to music and

play on my computer,' Justin replied. 'Mark lent me a new game.'

'Lucky you,' said his mum, handing him a large plate of pizza and salad. 'Before you go to bed, make sure you put those new trainers away properly,' she reminded him.

He looked across at them and smiled. The black leather seemed to shine.

'*Of course* I will,' he grinned.

Justin dozed happily in bed, the images of scoring the winning goal for Liverpool in the Champions League Cup Final still vivid. He would go down in history! '*Jus-tin. Jus-tin,*' the crowd roared in his dream.

'*Jus-tin!*'

He turned over.

'*Justin!*'

His eyes snapped open as he realized this was no dream. His name *was* being shouted, but not by fifty thousand delighted Liverpool fans.

It was his mum.

'All right, Mum!' Justin yelled back as he clambered out of bed. 'I'm up!'

Justin glanced at the clock on his bedside table and noticed that it was almost eleven in the morning. No wonder his mum was calling. He was late for school!

Moving with remarkable speed considering he was still half asleep, Justin struggled into his school shirt and trousers and hurtled down the stairs, skidding breathlessly into the living-room where his mum was standing, hands firmly on hips.

'Why didn't you wake me up earlier, Mum?' Justin asked, his head getting caught in his shirt sleeve. 'I'll probably get a detention for this.'

'For what?' his mum asked, irritably.

'For being late,' he said, eventually losing his balance and tumbling back into an armchair.

His mum stared at him for a moment, and then sighed. 'Justin, it's Saturday.'

He was about to start complaining about being woken up so early in that case. But then his brain registered the anger in his mum's tone.

She marched over to the living-room window. 'Do you know anything about this?' she demanded, pointing out to the front garden.

Justin rose from the chair and went to see. He surveyed the scene with complete bewilderment. Several of the plants at the edges of the largest flower-bed had been crushed. Petals floated mournfully on the mild breeze.

'You *know* how much trouble I take over the garden,' his mum said through gritted teeth. 'You've been jumping over the flower-beds again, haven't you? I know you do it, Justin. I've seen you!'

'Mum, I didn't touch them,' Justin protested.

His mum marched him outside. 'Then what are these?' she demanded, pointing to some shoe imprints close to one of the obliterated plants.

The prints were exactly the same shape and size

as those of Justin's new trainers. He was so surprised, he didn't know what to say.

His mum sighed. 'I thought you'd be honest enough to tell me if you'd damaged my flowers, Justin,' she said, sounding disappointed in him. 'This is just not like you. I want this mess tidied up right now.'

'But, Mum—'

'No buts – *now*, Justin,' his mum insisted. 'Go upstairs and change into some old clothes – you've got a lot of clearing up to do.'

Justin could tell that his mum was close to tears. She was upset as well as angry. It was a lethal combination and he knew there was no way she was going to listen to him.

He skulked upstairs, walked over to his bed and reached beneath it for his new trainers. He hadn't ruined his mum's flower-bed – he knew that for a fact. He'd come home from playing football, he'd had some dinner, cleaned the new trainers and gone to bed. In fact, he'd specifically decided *not* to jump the flower-beds!

As he pulled the trainers out from under the bed, Justin gasped. He felt the hairs at the back of his neck rise and goose bumps appear on his skin.

The black leather upper and silver-grey laces of his new trainers were stained with mud, and earth was smeared on the jagged white stripe that adorned their sides. Worst of all, between the laces on the left trainer was a single red petal.

No – this can't be right, Justin thought to himself. But his mum would never believe it wasn't him if she saw his trainers like this.

Justin knew *he* hadn't put his new trainers on and caused the damage. But, if *he* hadn't, then who had? Could someone have sneaked into the house while he was sleeping and taken the trainers? The thought of someone creeping unnoticed into his bedroom was even scarier than his mum's rage.

The more Justin thought about it, the more it unsettled him. Someone must have come into his room while he was asleep, put on his new trainers,

93

destroyed his mum's flower-beds and then returned the trainers again.

Justin swallowed hard. Why would anyone want to do that?

'Justin!'

The sound of his name startled him.

'I'm doing washing,' his mum called up the stairs. 'If you've got anything that needs doing, then get it out now, please.'

'Hang on!' he blurted, hurtling from his room and heading into the bathroom, the trainers still clutched in his hand. He locked the bathroom door behind him.

'Did you hear me, Justin?' his mum persisted.

He heard footsteps on the stairs.

'I said I need your dirty washing,' she said as she continued on up to the landing.

Justin turned on the taps in the sink. 'Yeah, I know, Mum, I'll be with you in a minute,' he called. He pushed the left trainer under the taps and began washing away the mud.

'What are you doing in there?' his mum asked, tapping on the bathroom door. 'Are you all right?'

Justin finished cleaning the left trainer and then frantically started working on the right one. 'Nothing, I'm fine!' he shouted back, trying to wipe away mud from the plug hole. 'Just had to run to the loo. Must have been that pizza we had last night.'

He hastily dried the trainers with toilet roll then flushed the soggy sheets away, breathing hard. The trainers were resting on the sink, the leather gleaming and the laces clean once again.

'I'm not waiting any longer – bring your washing with you when you come back down,' his mum called impatiently. 'I'll be in the garden.'

Justin stared at the trainers and then hurried back into his room with them and stuffed them out of sight under his bed. Grabbing his dirty washing, he made his way down the stairs and dropped it on top of the washing-machine on his way out into the back garden, where his mum was waiting.

She nodded in the direction of a broom and rake. 'I'll leave you to it,' she said, heading off back into the house. 'And you can forget about going swimming until that mess is cleaned up.'

'Mum . . .' Justin began, but she closed the back door on his protests.

Grumbling to himself, Justin picked up the rake and began pulling it over the earth in the flower-bed.

'What have you been doing this time?'

The voice made Justin look up. Peering over the low hedge that separated Justin's garden from the house next door was the gaunt, sour face of Mr Wilson, a man in his late fifties who lived there alone.

Justin sighed. This was the last thing he needed now.

'Been causing trouble again, have you?' Mr Wilson continued, looking Justin up and down and shaking his head.

'I didn't do anything, Mr Wilson,' Justin told him.

'I heard your mother,' Mr Wilson said, watching him. 'Why would you want to go and ruin her flower-beds?'

'I didn't!' Justin denied hotly, returning to his raking.

'Kids like you have got no respect for anything these days,' Mr Wilson continued. 'The only thing you care about is yourselves.'

Justin gripped the rake more tightly, trying to shut out the unfair comments. The heat of the morning sun beating down on the back of his neck wasn't helping his mood, and Mr Wilson's unkind words were making things ten times worse. Justin could feel his anger rising with the temperature.

'Bad kids like you need a father to keep them under control,' Mr Wilson declared. 'Otherwise they just run riot.' He paused to look Justin up and down, and then shook his head. 'No wonder your father ran off and left you,' he added, with a loud tut.

Justin threw down the rake. Now he was furious.

'My dad didn't run off,' he snapped, taking a step towards the fence. 'It was just that he and Mum didn't get along any more. It happens,' he finished, through gritted teeth.

Mr Wilson took a step backwards. 'Don't you touch me!' he exclaimed, raising his hands as if to defend himself. They were flecked with yellow paint. He'd been painting his front door, window frames and garage door a sickly shade of yellow. 'I'll tell your mother you threatened me – you're nothing more than a little thug!' he hissed.

Justin was about to answer back, but then he noticed his mum looking through the living-room window. She jabbed a finger in the direction of the flower-bed, as if to remind him of his task.

Justin swallowed hard, picked up the rake and sucked in a deep breath.

'Thinking of hitting me with that, are you?' Mr Wilson accused, pointing at the rake.

Justin lowered his head for a moment, fighting to

gain control of his temper. He remembered a trick his dad had taught him to cope with anger: if someone was getting on your nerves or annoying you, just imagine them with a bag on their head. Paper, plastic or canvas. Plain or patterned. It didn't matter. He looked up and saw that Mr Wilson was still scowling at him over the fence. Justin stared back, imagining Mr Wilson with a crumpled brown paper bag on his head. A smile found its way on to Justin's face.

'What are you grinning at?' Mr Wilson demanded suspiciously.

'Nothing, Mr Wilson,' Justin answered, returning to his raking. 'Nothing at all . . .' His secret made him smile even more.

The ringing of a phone drifted on the warm air and Mr Wilson turned and disappeared inside his house.

'That's it,' Justin murmured to himself. 'Go and answer your phone. It might be the Prime Minister telling you when to collect your Nasty Neighbour of the Year Award.' He sighed, and continued with his raking.

By the time Justin had tidied up the mess in the garden and had joined his friends to go swimming, he'd managed to put most of the unpleasant exchange with Mr Wilson out of his mind. They got changed, then hurried out to the pool area, where they dived, laughing, into the water.

They spent more than an hour in the pool, talking in between racing each other up and down. Paul won the breath-holding contest, but Mark managed to pip both of them in their final race.

The three friends climbed out of the water and headed back towards the changing room, but their laughter died abruptly as they entered. The doors to all three of their lockers were wide open. Their sports bags had been pulled out on to the wet, tiled floor and were gaping open, the contents strewn about. Two pairs of trainers had been flung into the corner.

'Look at my T-shirt!' Mark protested, picking up the sodden, crumpled garment. 'My mum'll go mad when she sees it. It was a birthday present!'

'It looks like someone's trodden on them,' Paul muttered, holding up his jeans and inspecting the wet footprints on the material. He stuffed a hand into one of the pockets. 'And I had five pounds in there,' he groaned. 'Someone's taken it.'

Justin moved towards his own open locker, his heart thumping hard.

He peered inside.

Though his clothes had also been strewn about, his new trainers were still in there, side by side. He lifted them up and saw that the soles were wet. There was something stuck to the bottom of the left trainer. It was a five pound note.

Justin felt as if someone had pumped icy water into his veins.

First the damage to his mum's garden – and now this. Was someone following him? Putting on his new trainers and causing trouble so that he would get the blame?

But *why*? Who would *want* to?

Justin tried to think if he had offended or annoyed anyone. But, even if he *had*, would they go as far as this to get back at him?

His mind spinning, Justin grabbed the five pound note and screwed it up in his hand, hoping no one had seen it stuck to his trainer. Not knowing how to explain how he came to have it, he hurriedly picked up his own jeans from the wet floor and pushed the five pound note into one of the pockets. He'd have to think of a way to smuggle it back to Paul without him knowing.

'Did they damage or take anything of yours, Justin?' Mark wanted to know, still sounding annoyed about his T-shirt.

Justin shook his head and, without looking at his friends, he set about retrieving the rest of his scattered and damp clothes.

After pulling them on, Justin stepped into his

trainers and bent to fasten them. As he finished tying the laces, he realized that he'd done them up too tight. He reached down again to loosen them.

They wouldn't budge. In fact, it felt as if the laces were *tightening*. He took his hands away and stood up straight, gingerly putting weight on first one and then the other foot. The feeling of tightness seemed to pass.

Justin relaxed a little. It must have been because the laces were wet, he reasoned.

'Lucky they didn't touch your new trainers, Justin,' Mark said as they prepared to leave.

Justin looked down at his gleaming footwear. 'Yes,' he said, quietly. 'Lucky.'

Monday came round again. Justin decided to wear his old trainers to school as it had rained on Sunday and he didn't want to get his new ones dirty again.

When he returned home, he noticed that something strange was happening next door. Two police cars were parked outside Mr Wilson's house, their blue lights turning silently. A number of people who lived in the street had ventured out to see what was happening.

Mr Wilson was out there, speaking to a policeman, who was scribbling hastily in his notebook. Another policeman was speaking into a two-way radio.

As Justin stared at his neighbour, Mr Wilson looked up and held his gaze.

Justin looked away – and caught sight of Mr Wilson's old car parked, as always, inside Mr Wilson's garage. Through the open garage doors, Justin saw that the car was covered from boot to bonnet with vivid splashes of paint, the same sickly yellow that Mr Wilson had been using. Paint tins lay on the floor of the garage, their contents spilled across the concrete and up the walls.

'Local vandals by the look of it,' he heard the policeman say into his radio. 'No. It doesn't look like robbery. Nothing taken. Just the paint splashed about. Probably someone with a grudge;

someone who doesn't like him. Odd really, looks like they trod in the paint and then walked all over the car!'

Justin froze as he heard this. Then he hurried past, pushing his bike up the short path to his own front door.

'Hello, love,' his mum called from the kitchen as Justin let himself in. 'Are the police still out there?'

'Yeah, they are!' he called back as he hurriedly made his way up the stairs.

He pushed open his bedroom door and walked straight over to his bed. He'd left the new trainers under it. Dropping to his knees, he pulled them out.

There was yellow paint on the soles.

Justin shut his eyes tight, his entire body feeling as if it had suddenly been wrapped in a wet blanket.

He stood up and walked over to his wardrobe, then opened the doors and hurled the trainers inside. Then he slammed the door shut, his breath coming in short gasps.

This is crazy! he thought. *Who . . . what . . . is doing this?*

Justin stood with his back against the wardrobe door. *Why? In case it suddenly flies open and the trainers come hurtling out?* he asked himself, mockingly.

Shaking his head, he went back downstairs to fetch some paint stripper and an old cloth from the garden shed.

As Justin went through the kitchen he was relieved to hear his mum was now on the phone in the lounge. She wouldn't ask any awkward questions.

Justin sat on his bedroom floor, working off the sticky yellow paint from his trainers with the paint stripper and cloth. The fumes from the paint stripper made his eyes water and he got up to open a window.

As he worked he pondered on what to do next. *I need to find a way to stop the trainers being taken*, he thought to himself. He looked around the room. His wardrobe had a key – and there wasn't a spare. *That's it!* he thought.

When Justin had finished, he placed the trainers in the bottom of the wardrobe, shut the door firmly and turned the key. *No one's getting to those*, he said to himself, placing the key in the front pocket of his jeans.

For three days, Justin kept the trainers locked away until the paint stripper smell had disappeared. When his mum asked him why he wasn't wearing them, he said he was saving them for special occasions. Mark and some of his other friends asked him too, and he gave them the same excuse.

Justin went round to Mark's house to return the computer game he'd lent him.

'Where are the wonder trainers?' Mark asked jokily. 'I'd wear them all the time if they were mine,' he said, switching channels on the portable television in his room. He looked down at Justin's feet again. 'Your old ones are rubbish.'

Justin laughed. 'So are yours,' he replied.

'Yeah, but I haven't got any new ones to wear!' Mark replied.

Justin nodded, and then took a deep breath. 'Mark, this is going to sound stupid,' he began. 'Ever since I got those trainers some really weird things have been happening. I think someone's trying to get me into trouble.'

'What do you mean?' Mark asked, a curious look on his face.

'I found the new trainers with mud on them after my mum's flower-bed got trashed. I know I didn't do that,' Justin told him. 'And you know when we were at the swimming-pool? I found that five pound note Paul had stolen from his jeans pocket stuck to the bottom of one of my new trainers.'

'But Paul found the money in his jacket pocket later on,' Mark replied.

Justin shook his head. 'I put it there when he wasn't looking,' he confessed. 'And that's not all: after that, our neighbour, Mr Wilson's car got covered in paint footprints – and I found yellow paint on the soles of my new trainers!'

Mark whistled. 'Maybe it's the person who went into SportCity after you did,' he suggested. 'They must be jealous that you got in there before them as SportCity's ten thousandth customer.' Mark scratched his head thoughtfully. 'But that would mean they've been following you around – and would have had to sneak into your house to take the trainers, and then to put them back, without being noticed – on two separate occasions!'

'I know! It seems impossible – but how else could this have been happening?' Justin said frustratedly.

'Mate – I have no idea,' Mark replied, shrugging his shoulders.

'Anyway,' Justin went on, 'I think I may have solved the problem: I've locked the trainers in my wardrobe, so whoever's—'

'Wait a minute,' Mark interrupted, pointing at the television screen. 'I recognize that bloke!'

Justin turned to see a local news report had just

flashed on to the screen. 'He works – worked – at SportCity,' he told Mark. 'I remember seeing him when I got my new trainers.'

Mark turned up the volume. The voice of the newsreader filtered into the room.

'Police are urgently seeking information following a vicious attack on a local man inside his own home,' the newsreader announced. *'The man, who is in his thirties, is critically ill in hospital after sustaining severe injuries. He was repeatedly kicked. A police spokesman said there were no witnesses, and the man seems unable to give a description of his attacker. The alarm was raised when blood-soaked footprints were spotted around the man's front door.'*

Justin jumped to his feet, his face pale.

'What's the matter with you?' Mark asked.

'You heard what they said, Mark,' Justin gasped. 'What if it's the trainers again?' He turned towards the door. 'I've got to go,' he told Mark.

'Justin!' Mark called, but Justin was already running out of the room.

He jumped on to his bike and headed out on to

the road, pedalling furiously, his mind racing as fast as his legs. If locking the trainers away hadn't worked then what would? And who would be the next victim?

It was beginning to grow dark as Justin arrived home. His heart was pounding with the effort of cycling so fast, but also with the fear of what he might find there.

There were no lights on in the house.

Justin left his bike lying on the path and paused beside the front door, his hand shaking as he put the key into the lock.

The door swung back on its hinges as he stepped into the hall and reached for the light switch nearby.

'Mum?' he called nervously.

She didn't reply.

He walked in slowly. 'Mum!' he called again. This time it was louder and more urgent. Still no one replied.

She should be home, Justin thought, and panic rose inside him.

He turned into the living-room but there was no sign of her. He moved back into the hall and then on towards the kitchen.

'Mum,' Justin said once more, his voice wavering.

The kitchen door was shut and Justin gritted his teeth as he prepared to open it, terrified of what he might find on the other side.

Slowly, he pushed the door open and felt for the light switch.

The shadows in the kitchen vanished and Justin immediately spotted a knife lying on the kitchen table. The tip of the blade was stained with red.

Crimson drops decorated the worktop and the floor.

Justin grabbed the edge of the table, feeling dizzy and sick. His skin prickled and it felt as if cold arms were hugging him tightly. Then he heard a noise from above him.

A sharp creaking.

He headed back out into the hall, heart thundering against his ribs. For long seconds he stood there at the bottom of the stairs looking up into the blackness beyond the landing, wanting to know who was up there, but terrified of what he might find.

'Mum,' he called again, wanting so badly to hear her voice. 'Mum, is that you up there? Are you all right?'

Silence.

Trying to control his breathing, Justin put his foot on the first step and began to make his way upstairs.

He was halfway up when the hall light flickered for a second and then went out. Justin paused, the fear now a tight fist in his stomach.

It was dark downstairs and up now. But he knew he had to hurry on.

Reaching the top, he crossed the landing towards his bedroom. The door was ajar, but not quite enough for him to see inside.

He pushed it open, now barely able to control his escalating fear.

As far as he could see in the half-light, everything

in his room looked normal. Until he noticed a crimson trickle leaking out from behind the door of his wardrobe.

His hand shaking, Justin felt in his pocket. The wardrobe key was still there.

He crossed the room and pulled the handle of the wardrobe door. It came open.

The coppery odour of blood filled his nostrils.

Justin looked down to see his new trainers lying neatly together in the bottom of his wardrobe. The laces were soaked red, the insteps and soles drenched, some of the blood drying darkly around the toes.

Justin felt his stomach contract and he closed his eyes. For a second, he thought he was going to vomit. But after a few deep breaths he forced himself to open his eyes to examine the lock. It seemed to have been forced open.

From the inside.

For the first time, Justin wondered whether maybe there *hadn't* been anyone following him, taking the trainers to do terrible things in them so that Justin would get the blame. Maybe the trainers were doing terrible things all by themselves.

Maybe they were haunted . . . *possessed* . . .

How else could the happenings be explained?

Justin looked down at the trainers again.

So much blood.

Whose was it? The man who had been attacked? Whose?

His mum's?

His mind spinning, Justin rushed into his mum's room.

She wasn't there.

Nor in the bathroom.

Justin headed again for the stairs, then froze as he heard the front door open. He listened as the intruder made their way along the hall, wondering if he would be able to escape and raise the alarm.

'Just what I need! A blown fuse!'

Justin fell against the wall in relief as he heard his

mum's voice. And then the hall and stairs were flooded with light.

'That's better!' Justin's mum said.

Justin slammed his bedroom door shut behind him and then ran downstairs into the kitchen.

'Mum!' he gasped, rushing up to her. 'Are you all right?'

'Yes, I'm fine,' she told him, looking down in surprise at this unexpectedly powerful display of affection. 'You'll never believe it. I was chopping some onions and I cut my finger.' She held up the finger to show him. 'Bled like billy-o – and we didn't have any plasters left! So I had to nip to the shops and buy some.'

She frowned. 'Are you OK, Justin? You look as if you've seen a ghost.'

'I'm all right,' he lied. 'I got home and you weren't here. I was worried.' He managed a weak smile.

'Well I'm here now,' his mum told him. 'But I'm afraid dinner's going to be a bit late.'

'That's OK, Mum. I've got some cleaning up to do

in my room,' Justin told her. 'I er . . . spilled something on the carpet . . .' He turned and headed back out of the kitchen.

His mum raised her eyebrows in surprise. '*You* are going to do some cleaning up? Are you sure you're all right?' she joked.

Justin tried to smile, but he couldn't. He climbed the stairs slowly towards his room.

He rinsed the blood from the trainers in the bathroom sink, and then went to wipe up the blood from the base of his wardrobe. As he did so, Justin looked down at his red-stained fingers and thought about taking the trainers to the police.

And what would they say? Would they believe that he was bringing in evidence for them? No. They'd think he was confessing. Showing them the proof of his crime. They were *his* trainers after all. *His* trainers that were covered in blood. What was he going to say to them?

'Excuse me but these trainers may well have killed someone. I think you'd better arrest them and send them to prison.'

Justin knew he had to get rid of the trainers. He'd never been more certain of anything in his life. He found a plastic bag and jammed the new trainers inside.

He decided he would take them to the local dump in the morning. He'd hurl them as far away as possible and leave them to rot with the rest of the rubbish. That would do it.

Justin woke suddenly from a troubled night's sleep. With a heavy heart, he looked over to the bag containing his new trainers and then swung himself out of bed and pulled back the curtains. The windows were spattered with rain, and trickles of it chased down the glass like tears.

He dressed quickly and put on his old trainers. Picking up the bag containing his new ones, Justin made his way downstairs.

He could hear his mum moving about in the kitchen. 'Won't be long, Mum!' he called.

His mum came rushing out. 'Where are you going

without any breakfast – and why are you wearing those rotten, smelly old things?' she asked, pointing down at Justin's old trainers. 'Put those nice new ones on and come and eat your breakfast before you go!' she insisted. And then she disappeared back into the kitchen.

Justin sat down on the bottom step of the staircase and opened the plastic bag. Reluctantly, he took the new trainers out and slipped them on, fastening the laces loosely. He might as well wear them one last time. He'd take his old trainers with him to the dump and change back into them before chucking the new ones. He'd just have to deal with his mum's complaints when he came home without his new trainers later.

With his old trainers in the plastic bag, Justin walked towards the town dump. But he was having difficulty. When he'd played football in the trainers they'd seemed to give him speed he'd never possessed before. However, now it was an effort even to raise his foot off the pavement. It felt as if someone had lined the trainers with lead.

Now that he was out of his mum's sight, Justin decided to put on his old trainers now rather than at the dump. He bent down to undo the new trainers. Immediately, the laces tightened and the trainers gripped his feet like an eagle's claws gripping on prey.

This time there was no denying it.

The trainers had their own free will.

Feeling icy with fear, Justin realized he had no choice but to fight the trainers and carry on with his plan to get rid of them.

Wincing with pain, he forced himself to walk on, every step an effort.

Normally it would have taken him less than ten minutes to run from his house to the dump, but there was *nothing* normal about this journey. A few metres further on, Justin's right foot was suddenly yanked violently to one side, almost causing him to overbalance. With a massive effort, he managed to remain on the pavement.

The other trainer plunged forwards, once again twisting his torso and making him cry out in pain.

He looked down at the trainers and gritted his teeth in concentration. 'No,' he hissed, trying to prevent the movement again. But he may as well have been a marionette, dancing on the strings of some mad puppeteer. He had no control over his limbs.

He winced as pain shot from his right ankle and up his calf. It felt as if someone had grabbed his foot and twisted it savagely. Then he yelled out as his left knee was yanked just as sharply. He gripped the knee-cap, fearing that it would burst. Fire burned in his legs as the joints were forced this way and that, twisted into impossible positions by the trainers.

A man was coming towards him.

'Help me!' Justin called, waving frantically at the man, who just glanced at him as if he was mad and walked on.

Justin tried again when a car passed by, but the driver also looked at him, shook his head and drove on.

With sweat dripping into his eyes, Justin realized that he was only a hundred metres or so from the dump now. If he could just keep going . . .

But six lanes of traffic separated him from the end of his journey.

'Come on!' he snarled, glaring down at his feet.

A car hurtled past close to him, the slipstream ruffling his hair. Justin gasped as he realized how close to the kerb he was.

The laces of the trainers tightened so hard he yelled out in agony, but his shout was drowned by the noise of the traffic speeding back and forth along the wide road. He tried to block out the terrible throbbing pain.

Suddenly, the trainers seemed to give up the fight.

Justin sucked in a deep breath and ran, darting across the road as quickly as he could. As he got to the middle lane, he stopped dead, his feet jammed to the Tarmac.

He felt a wave of pure terror as he looked frantically around and saw a car bearing down on him. The trainers had taken over again. He was stranded.

He heard its horn blaring and watched the driver gesturing wildly at him to move.

But he couldn't.

At the final moment, the car swerved, missing him by a hair's breadth.

There was another behind it. Then a motorbike. Both vehicles swept around him.

Justin gritted his teeth and stood still, his heart pounding hard against his ribs.

Keep calm, Justin told himself. *Concentrate. The cars won't hit you. They can see you standing here.*

The police station was on the other side of the road. Perhaps someone inside would hear the sound of blaring hooters, see him stuck in the traffic, and come out and help. Justin hoped so. He was prepared to be told off for trying to cross such a busy road, endangering himself and disrupting traffic. He just needed someone to help him.

Again he tried to move when there was a gap in the stream of onrushing vehicles, but it was useless.

Sweat was now pouring down his face. With a huge effort, he forced his feet forwards, the traffic still roaring past him on both sides. He moved forward a couple of steps. Another few metres and he'd be on the opposite pavement.

The blaring of horns from so many different vehicles built into a deafening symphony of noise that threatened to burst Justin's eardrums.

Then again, the trainers stopped him in his tracks. A white van swept past him. Justin closed his eyes in terror.

There was a loud blaring to his left – much louder than a car horn.

Justin opened his eyes to see a lorry thundering towards him in the middle lane.

He was rooted to the spot.

The lorry driver sounded his air horn again, the noise drumming in Justin's ears, the huge, gleaming radiator grille like the bared teeth of a hungry predator.

Justin saw the face of the lorry driver, teeth gritted in desperation, as he spun the wheel in a desperate effort to avoid him. The lorry swung to the left, narrowly missing an oncoming car. The huge front tyres shrieked as their rubber burned along the Tarmac.

Still, Justin couldn't move.

He looked down at the trainers with utter desperation.

And then he was hurtled into the air as if yanked by invisible ropes. The breath was torn from his lungs. He didn't even have the chance to scream as he landed back in the path of the lorry.

All he saw was the onrushing mountain of metal, knowing with terrible clarity that, this time, the lorry was going to hit him.

*   *   *

The shrill whine of police and ambulance sirens filled the air with their banshee wail as emergency vehicles roared past towards the scene of carnage.

The two lads hadn't seen what had happened. They had seen the titanic explosion, like a shrieking ball of fire. A huge black mushroom cloud of smoke had risen from the blast and now hovered above the scene like a monstrous, heaving curtain. Another onlooker had murmured that the blast had been caused by a car running into the back of the braking lorry and rupturing its fuel tank.

The lads stood mesmerized by the mass of traffic that had come to a halt across all three lanes of the road.

One of them noticed something lying in the gutter a few metres away. He went over for a closer look.

'Hey, look at these!' he said, calling his friend over.

Lying by the kerb was a pair of trainers. The soles were virtually unmarked and the tops looked as if they'd been freshly scrubbed.

'They're cool,' said the other lad. 'Who'd want to leave them here?'

'Someone must have just thrown them away,' his friend said. 'They look about your size. Try them on. They're just like mine, the ones I got from SportCity a couple of weeks ago.'

The other lad took off his old trainers and slipped on the new ones. 'A perfect fit,' he said, smiling.

AN APPLE
A DAY

Tim Barnett was beginning to wonder if a person could melt if the sun was too hot.

He wiped sweat from his face and glanced up at the cloudless blue sky. The sun had been shining since he'd woken that morning. In fact, it had been shining ever since Tim had arrived at his gran's farm three days ago – not that he was complaining. He loved the hot weather, and with another nine days to go before his parents came to pick him up, he hoped the sun would continue to shine as brightly as it was shining now.

Tim cycled along the narrow dirt track, stopping occasionally to peer across the fields that stretched away in all directions. The grass and weeds on either side of the track were almost as high as his waist, and the fields beyond were equally overgrown.

He rounded a slight bend, and the farm and its outbuildings came back into view. As well as the farmhouse itself, there was a barn, a milking shed, some stables, a garage where the tractor had been stored and a couple of old, rusted pigpens – long since abandoned. Pieces of disused farmyard equipment dotted the main yard and the areas nearby like the rusted skeletons of metallic dinosaurs. All untouched since his grandad's death.

Over the years, during his many visits to Gran's, Tim had explored the entire farm. The barn in particular had proved to be full of amazing stuff; old farm tools like huge scythes and rusted sickles were propped up everywhere like the disused weapons of some strange army. Tim liked the stillness in there and, when the weather got unbearably hot, it was pleasant and cool inside, with its high roof and long, splintered shadows.

The barn was also home to one of the largest spiders he'd ever seen in his life. Its web was high up in the eaves of the barn, but Tim could still make out its eight-legged shape whenever it ventured forth to feast on its latest victim. Its massive webs were all over the barn. Tim had found the remains of flies, wasps and even other spiders in its silken traps. It was as if the spider was making the barn its own.

Grandad had died seven years earlier, when Tim was just four; he had only a few memories of him. Dad had tried to persuade Gran to come and live with them at their home in London but she'd said the farm had always been her home and she didn't intend leaving it. Well, what she'd actually said was, 'There's a place for everything and everything in its place.'

And later, when Tim's dad had tried to tell Gran that she might not be able to look after the place on her own, she'd smiled, saying, 'Don't judge a book by its cover.'

That was another one of her sayings. Gran had a saying for anything and everything and, if he was honest, Tim sometimes found them really irritating.

If he was up a little later than usual in the morning it was, 'Early to bed, early to rise, makes you healthy, wealthy and wise.'

If he ate too quickly, he was '. . . eating as if your belly thinks your throat's been cut.'

Gran was superstitious too. Not just about things like not walking under ladders – Tim knew all about that – but also about strange things he'd never heard of.

One night while they were eating their dinner, he'd reached across the table for the mashed potatoes and knocked over the salt shaker. Straight away, Gran had told him to throw a pinch of salt over his left shoulder.

'Why, Gran?' he'd asked her, laughing.

'To blind the Devil sitting on your shoulder,' she'd told him sternly, making sure he completed the strange ritual.

Tim had done as she'd told him, even though he'd thought the whole thing a bit weird, to say the least.

He was startled from his thoughts by a large black crow taking off from a nearby tree. Watching as the bird rose into the cloudless sky, Tim cycled onwards along one of the many overgrown pathways that crisscrossed the farmland like thick brown veins. He had discovered dozens of them during his visits, but he wondered how many more still lay hidden.

Approaching the farmhouse, Tim aimed for a dusty-looking patch of ground. He put down one foot and hit the rear brake, skidding dramatically to a halt. Clouds of dust rose into the dry air.

With a broad grin of satisfaction on his face, Tim looked up to see his gran standing in the doorway of the farmhouse clutching a large glass of lemonade.

'There's a cold drink here for you,' she said, smiling

at him through her large round glasses, the sun reflecting off her snow-white hair.

'Did you see how fast I was going, Gran?' Tim asked, gratefully receiving the drink from her and taking a huge gulp.

'Yes, I did. You want to be careful that you don't fall off.'

Tim rolled his eyes. 'Don't worry, Gran. You wait until you see what I've got planned for tomorrow,' he went on excitedly.

Gran looked up at the cloudless sky. 'Touch wood, the weather stays nice for you,' she said.

Tim rolled his eyes again. If he had a pound for every time he'd heard her say 'touch wood' when she was wishing for something, he could afford to buy those new trainers he wanted.

That evening, the two of them sat watching television together. Banjo, Gran's beagle, lay on the rug by the old open fireplace. Tim munched noisily on an apple from the fruit bowl on the lounge table.

'Watch out for the pips,' she told him, chuckling. 'Don't want a tree growing in your tummy!'

Tim laughed and took another bite. *Gran and her crazy sayings*, he thought.

There was a programme on about farming in the old days, and how it used to be big business. Tim watched with interest as the brown and white photos and film clips flashed across the screen one after another. 'Hey – that's exactly like the one in Grandad's barn!' he said, pointing at an old plough on the screen.

'You're right,' Gran replied. 'Your grandad used that plough for over thirty years. Even when new ones came along, he stuck with it. He said that just because it was old, it didn't mean that it was useless.'

Suddenly, Gran turned to Tim and held his hand tightly. 'I still miss your grandad, you know. But God moves in mysterious ways.' She relaxed her grip and searched for a tissue to dry her teary eyes. 'He must have thought it was your grandad's time.'

Tim gave his gran a comforting hug, and then turned back to the TV. But now all he could think about was how little he knew about his grandad's death. He had been told that Grandad had been killed in an accident on the farm. No one had ever spoken to him about the actual *details* of how Grandad had died, but then again, Tim reasoned, he had never really asked. Once, quite a long time ago, Tim had heard his mum and dad talking about it, when they thought that he was asleep. Dad had said that the accident had been unusual. Strange. And all Gran had said when Tim had asked her about it was, 'There are some things you're better off not knowing.'

The following morning, Tim was woken by sunlight streaming into his room. He yawned, stretched and leaped out of bed. As he made his way across the small landing to the bathroom, he could hear Gran preparing breakfast in the kitchen below. He washed and dressed, then hurried downstairs.

'Here's a nice bacon sandwich for you,' his gran said.

'Thanks, Gran!' Eager to make the most of the fine weather, Tim loaded his roll up with tomato ketchup and tucked into it, washing it down with a cup of tea. Swallowing the last mouthful, he took his plate and cup over to the sink.

'Hurry along outside, then,' his gran said with a smile. 'It'd be a shame to miss out on any of this sunshine.'

Tim grinned at her. Sometimes she seemed to read his thoughts!

'You know what they say,' she called as Tim hurried out and clambered on to his bike. 'The early bird catches the worm!'

'Yes, and it's a good job you touched wood yesterday when you wished for sunshine, Gran!' he called back.

Tim rode off across the yard. There was a sudden rush of movement ahead of him, and Banjo came hurtling into view, barking and wagging his tail excitedly.

'Come on, you nutter,' he chuckled, as the beagle came bounding over to him. Tim turned his bike around and began pedalling as hard as he could, with Banjo sprinting along beside him. The beagle loved having Tim around to play with.

The dirt track was deeply rutted in places, the ground baked hard by long weeks of sunshine. Tim had to grip his handlebars tightly. It was loads of fun – trying to keep his balance over the uneven terrain, while trying to go as fast as he could.

After a couple of hours' off-roading, Tim arrived back at the farm with an exhausted beagle at his heels. He had a cool drink and a snack, and then looked around for something to occupy the afternoon.

'Bingo,' he said to himself as he remembered the planks of wood and rusted old oil-drums near the back of the barn. He busied himself heaving the empty old drums into the open and propping up a couple of the planks of wood against them so that they sloped upwards like a ramp.

'What are you doing now, Tim?' His gran's voice drifted across to him on a warm breeze as she emerged from the farmhouse, a basketful of washing under one arm.

'I'm going to jump that,' Tim told her, nodding towards the makeshift ramp.

'Look before you leap,' his gran said, shaking her head as she hung a long white sheet on the line.

Tim puffed out his chest. 'I've looked, and I'll do it easily,' he told her. 'I'm a great cyclist.'

Gran tutted. 'Pride comes before a fall,' she answered, bending down to pick up more pegs.

Tim shook his head then set off, pedalling frantically. He'd show her – her and her daft old sayings.

Speeding towards the wooden ramp, Tim braced himself for impact. Nearby, Banjo barked in expectation.

Suddenly, Tim felt something tugging at his ankle. Looking down, he realized with horror that his sock had snagged in the bike's chain. He panicked as the bike hit the base of the ramp. He was losing control.

The bike veered to one side and Tim felt himself falling. He vaguely heard his gran shout somewhere behind him just before he hit the ground hard and rolled, his momentum carrying him towards the hedge that separated the farmhouse garden from the yard. He slid into it feet first, thorns digging into his skin and stinging nettles lashing at his hands. The bike cartwheeled through the air and landed loudly close by.

'Tim! Are you all right?' his gran cried, putting down the laundry basket and hurrying over.

Tim groaned and attempted to pull himself free, wincing as pieces of thorn bush grazed his bare legs and arms.

'Come on, you,' Gran said, appearing next to him. 'I told you to be careful, didn't I?' She shook her head. 'You're always in too much of a hurry,' she scolded. 'More haste, less speed, that's what they say.'

'Who are *they*, Gran?' Tim asked, glaring down at his torn sock and the scraped skin underneath it, and then at his overturned bike. '*They* seem to know everything. Do *they* sit around in a room making these things up just so people can repeat them?' He picked himself up, grabbed his bike, pulled some leaves from his hair and stalked off in the direction of the barn.

Tim wasn't sure how long he'd been in the rickety old barn. All he wanted to do was to be on his own in the cool, and nurse his injured pride without his gran going on at him.

'Dinner in quarter of an hour!' he heard her shout from the farmhouse.

Tim was surprised to hear her call out, as he hadn't realized how late it had got. 'Hmph. Not hungry,' he mumbled to himself, tearing a piece of straw in two.

His stomach grumbled, and he knew that his body didn't agree. He was, in fact, famished, and it didn't help that there was a delicious smell wafting from the kitchen that he recognized – it was one of Gran's apple pies. Tim's mouth watered, but he wasn't ready to face her just yet. Though his cuts stung a little bit, it was his pride that had taken the real bashing. He decided to find something else to eat; he didn't know where from, but he was determined that he would.

Tim walked to the barn door and peered out. The sun was sinking slowly on the horizon, and clouds of midges hung in the air like winged cinders. Leaving his bike resting against the cracked wooden wall, he slipped out of the barn and across the yard.

There was a small copse of trees lined with hedges away to his right and he headed for those. Perhaps he could find some blackberries, to stave off his hunger.

As he picked his way through the foliage, he came to a high stone wall ahead. Up until now, most of it had been masked by tall, thickly overgrown brambles that had prevented him from getting close enough to see what was on the other side. But most of those bushes had withered in the heat. Curiosity made him forget his hunger for a moment, as he wondered what lay beyond it.

There were a couple of fallen trees nearby, and Tim hurried towards them. By climbing on the gnarled trunks, he'd be able to see over the wall.

The sight that met his eyes when he reached the top made him gasp. Beyond the wall was a huge orchard. It seemed to stretch away for miles. And every one of the trees in it was laden with ripe and juicy-looking red apples.

Tim prepared to hoist himself up. A quick jump down, grab a couple of the apples, and then out again. Simple.

He knew that the apples weren't his, but whoever owned this orchard had thousands of apples and they wouldn't miss a few, would they?

Tim swung himself up on to the wall, braced himself for a moment and then dropped on to the soft grass that carpeted the orchard. He got to his feet and looked around him.

This was like no orchard Tim had ever seen. Every tree was pretty much the same height, with the same large split in the trunk that forked into two largish branches which, in turn, split into yet smaller branches. Tim was staggered at the amount of apples on each branch. It was a miracle that they didn't break under the weight!

He wandered slowly between the trees, aware that twilight was turning to darkness, but mesmerized by the sight of so much ripe fruit – it all looked so perfect. After a while, he found a piece of fallen branch. He swung it at the lowest limb of the nearest tree, cracking it hard against the wood.

No apples fell.

Tim struck again, and the sound resounded through the orchard like a gunshot.

'Hey, you!'

The shout came from somewhere to his left, piercing the gloom. Tim looked around for its source.

'Get out of my orchard!' the voice roared.

At last, Tim saw where the words were coming from. A figure was moving quickly towards him through the semi-darkness. Tim could just make out that it was a large, white-bearded man, and it looked as though he was carrying a shotgun.

'Get out of here!' the man bellowed.

Tim turned and ran. His fear seemed to give him extra speed but, in the gloom of the twilight, it was difficult to see. He tripped over a fallen branch and went sprawling.

As he rolled over, desperately trying to regain his balance, he saw that the man was drawing nearer, his great white beard like a threatening beacon in the dull, early-evening light. The orchard wall was about twenty metres ahead.

Tim scrambled to his feet, aware that he'd scraped one knee, but frantic to be out of the reach of this crazy old man.

Fifteen metres.

He ran on, ducking to avoid colliding with

a low tree branch, then glancing behind him again.

The man was gaining on him.

Ten.

Tim flung himself at the wall, rough and dusty against his sweaty face. His fingers clawed desperately, trying to find the top, trying with all his strength to lever himself up. He felt himself losing his grip and shouted out in fear as he slipped and fell backwards, crashing into the soft grass. He turned to see the figure looming out of the trees.

'I told you to get out of my orchard!' snarled the old man.

Tim took another run at the wall and, this time, managed to get a good grip. He hauled himself up, trying to hook one leg over so that he could drop down safely to the other side, but he realized to his horror that he couldn't move. The toe of one of his old, tattered trainers was wedged in a gap in the wall.

Below him, the old man slowly raised the shotgun

to his shoulder. Tim could see a crooked smile on the face of the white-bearded figure.

'You've been warned, boy,' the old man rasped.

Tim tried to pull his foot free. His trainer remained wedged in the gap.

The old man had the shotgun pressed tightly against his shoulder now, and Tim realized in a heartbeat that he intended to fire.

'You should have kept away from here,' hissed the old man.

With a final despairing effort, Tim wrenched his trainer free. He slipped over the wall and fell heavily into the copse of trees on the other side, scrambling immediately to his feet.

'If you ever come back here, you'll be sorry!' roared the old man, his voice filling Tim's ears as it rose into the darkening sky.

Gasping for breath, Tim kept running, his heart hammering in his chest, looking over his shoulder, wondering if the man could have followed him over the wall. He didn't stop until he reached Gran's house.

He crashed through the kitchen door, almost colliding with the old oak table. Red-faced and shaking, he slumped down into one of the chairs.

His gran had been waiting for him. 'Where have you been?' she asked impatiently. 'I said quarter of an hour, Tim. Dinner is nearly spoiled. And it's your favourite – roast pork, followed by apple pie.'

Tim patted his belly and smiled in thanks as Gran took away his empty plate.

'Are you all right, Tim?' Gran asked. 'You've been quiet ever since you came in. Cat got your tongue?'

'No, I'm fine, Gran,' Tim said, the beating of his heart finally having returned to something like normal. 'Just enjoying my dinner, that's all. I didn't want to talk with my mouth full.'

'Quite right too, love. It's just that you looked a bit pale when you came in, that was all.' She put a slice of apple pie down in front of him.

The pie looked delicious, but the thought of apples suddenly sent a shiver of fear through Tim.

'Er . . . I think I'll skip the pie this time, Gran,' he said.

'But you love apple pie,' his gran remarked, surprised.

'I know, but I'm not really in the mood for it at the moment,' Tim mumbled.

'Well – it's up to you,' Gran said, taking the slice of pie away.

Tim took a sip of his lemonade. 'Gran,' he asked, sheepishly, 'you know that orchard that backs on to your farm – who does it belong to?'

'You keep away from there, Tim!' his gran warned, her expression suddenly anxious. 'That's owned by old Bill Cole. He's lived there on his own for as long as I can remember. He was there when I came to live on the farm with your grandad, and that was fifty years ago. Why do you ask?'

'I just wondered,' Tim said, deliberately not looking up at her.

'Don't you go getting curious about that place, Tim. Curiosity killed the cat, you know. And besides, old Bill Cole hates kids. They're always scrumping his apples and he'll do anything to stop them.'

Including pointing shotguns at them, Tim thought.

A sudden hammering on the front door startled them both.

'Who can that be at this time?' Gran said, wearily. She made her way out of the kitchen and along the hallway towards the front door.

Tim crept to the kitchen door and peered around it. As Gran opened the door he saw a terrifyingly familiar figure standing on the porch.

'Where's that boy?' Bill Cole hissed. 'The boy who was in my orchard!'

'I don't know what you're talking about, Mr Cole,' Gran replied. 'And I'll thank you not to talk to me in that tone. I'd like you to leave.'

'Not until I've done what I came here to do,' the old man snapped at her.

Tim stared with a mixture of fear and anger as old Bill Cole loomed in the doorway like a predator. *I have to help Gran*, he thought. He steeled himself and walked down the hall towards the front door.

Bill Cole's eyes narrowed as he caught sight of Tim. 'That's him! He was trying to steal my apples – just like the rest!'

'If Tim was in your orchard, Mr Cole, I'm sure he didn't mean any harm,' Gran said. 'Now will you *please* leave,' she repeated.

Bill Cole moved forward, ignoring Gran's words.

Though his heart was thumping in fear, Tim moved in front of his gran to protect her. 'Go AWAY!' he shouted. 'Who would want your rotten apples anyway?'

'What did you say, boy?' Bill Cole bellowed furiously.

'Hush, Tim, please,' Gran said quietly, drawing him to her.

Seeing the warning look in his gran's eyes, Tim shut up. But he was enraged with Bill Cole for being so rude and threatening to his gran.

'I'm sorry if you believe Tim was trying to steal your apples,' Gran went on.

'I'll make *him* sorry if he ever tries it again,' Bill Cole sneered. 'I don't want people coming near my land, you know that. Your husband knew that too, didn't he?' A hint of a smile played on Bill Cole's lips.

Tim felt his gran begin to tremble.

'But you're on *my* land at the moment,' she hit back, a tremor in her voice.

'You'd better get that boy under control or I'll deal with him myself,' Bill Cole snarled. 'Keep him away from my orchard *and* my apples.' He finally turned away.

Tim watched the old man slope off into the darkness. 'Are you all right, Gran?' he asked, taking her hand and leading her to a chair.

'I'm fine, Tim,' she told him, though he noticed that she was shaking ever so slightly. She reached into the pocket at the front of her apron with her free hand and pulled out a little lace handkerchief.

Tim watched as she dabbed quickly at the corners of both eyes. 'Somebody should do something about him, Gran,' he said angrily, squeezing her hand more tightly.

'Like what, Tim?' his gran sighed.

Banjo, sensing Gran's distress, ambled over and lay at her feet, glancing up with his big, watery eyes as if to check she was all right.

'Come on,' smiled Gran. '*Both* of you.' She leaned forward and stroked Banjo. 'I'm fine.'

'I heard what that man said. I *was* in his orchard but I didn't steal any of his apples, Gran. I promise.'

'I believe you, Tim,' she said, squeezing his hand. 'Don't you worry about him. He doesn't scare me. Your grandad always said he was a nasty piece of work.'

Tim stood up and puffed out his chest. 'I'm going to go after him and *tell* him I never touched his apples,' he muttered. '*And* I'm going to tell him that he was rude for talking to you like he did.'

'No, Tim,' his gran said quickly. 'Just leave it. It's over now. I'm fine.' She smiled up at him. 'Now, why don't you eat your apple pie? I baked it specially.

And you know what they say: "Waste not, want not".'

Tim did as he was asked – but by now, he was furious. As he ate, he thought about old Bill Cole. He shouldn't have been mean to Gran like that – she hadn't done anything. He was just a selfish old bully and it was time someone taught him a lesson.

Next morning, Tim was up early and out of the house before he'd even had his breakfast. With Gran still calling something to him about breakfast being the most important meal of the day, he hurried across to the barn and retrieved a rusted metal bucket which he hung over his handlebars.

Tim cycled as fast as he could towards the copse of trees and the high stone wall that lay beyond.

When he reached the wall, he hurled the bucket over and stood waiting to see if anyone came. When no one did, he scrambled to the top and waited. He heard nothing but the soft singing of birds.

Tim had a good view through the heavily laden apple trees in old Bill Cole's orchard and he could see that the farmhouse and wooden barn stood about one hundred metres to his left. He hadn't noticed this on his first foray into the orchard.

He dropped down into the orchard out of sight of the house and picked up the rusty bucket. He moved cautiously between the rows of apple trees – he didn't want to bump into Bill Cole.

As Tim drew nearer to the house, he was relieved to discover that the apple trees were planted closely enough for him to approach without being seen. He could hear a soft jingling sound nearby, and he looked more closely to see what was making the noise.

Hanging from the porch of the house and also from the doorway of the barn was a row of old, rusted wind chimes in the shape of large spiders, their metal legs chiming tinnily in the faint breeze. Tim stopped for a moment and watched the swaying shapes before ducking behind one of the trees nearby. He scrabbled around in the long, lush grass, and finally closed his fingers around a largish, flat stone. He then got up, took aim and threw it at old Bill Cole's house.

It struck the frame of the front door with a harsh crack. Tim waited, then threw another stone. This one hit the door dead centre.

Moments later, Bill Cole emerged, looking around, wild anger making his cheeks ruddy. 'Who's there?' he roared.

Tim was still ducked down behind the tree, trying not to breathe for fear of getting caught.

After a moment, Bill Cole disappeared back inside his house, and Tim moved nearer to the barn, where he picked up another stone. He threw this one as hard as he could, and again, it hit the front door.

Bill Cole was outside again in an instant, his beady dark eyes scanning the greenery for intruders. 'If that's you, boy, you'll be sorry,' he called.

Tim held his breath again. He could feel his heart beating through his shirt, and perspiration dotted his forehead.

'I know you can hear me,' Bill Cole continued.

'Well, your gran's not here to protect you now, is she? You heed my warning – don't eat what's not yours. You'll regret it.'

The old farmer dipped back inside the house for a moment and re-emerged, carrying his shotgun. He strode off across his yard into the rows of apple trees opposite where Tim was hiding.

Tim could hear him muttering irritably to himself as he stalked through the orchard, his voice gradually fading as he moved further and further away. Tim waited a moment longer then jumped and swung on the lowest branch of the tree nearest to him.

Red apples showered down around him, and he worked quickly gathering up as many as he could, placing them in the rusty bucket. Making sure that the old man wasn't around, he crept over to the next two trees and did the same thing; apples cascaded down, rolling here and there on the soft grassy carpet.

Once the bucket was full, Tim hurried over to the

porch of old Bill Cole's house and emptied the apples out on to the cracked wood, then he turned and sprinted back among the apple trees and gathered more apples into his bucket, which he once more deposited on to the old wooden porch.

The spider wind chimes twisted and clanked in the breeze every time he ran past them. Moving as quickly as he could, Tim repeated his movements until the porch of Bill Cole's house was nothing but a sea of red apples. He hurriedly moved apples left and right until he was satisfied with his work. He could still hear the old man shouting far away in the trees.

Tim retreated carefully back across the yard. He smiled to himself; the apples he'd arranged so carefully on the porch spelled out the word BULLY in large, red letters.

Perfect.

That's what you get for being so selfish and for shouting at my gran, he thought.

Tim ran into the nearby barn and looked around.

There was a ladder behind him leading up to a hayloft. He climbed it, and settled himself in a shadowy corner. He knew it was possible that Bill Cole would come looking in here – but he was confident that the dark shadows would hide him well.

The view was brilliant. BULLY was even more prominent from Tim's vantage point. From where he was hiding he had a good view of the entire orchard and, even better, of old Bill Cole stomping irritably back towards the house.

'I know there's someone here,' the old man shouted into the trees. Then his anger turned to surprise as he saw what Tim had spelled out using the fallen apples. Tim grinned to himself as he watched from the hayloft.

'How dare you!' the white-bearded old man roared. He stepped back but, as he did, he trod on one of the scattered apples and overbalanced.

Tim watched open-mouthed as Bill Cole pitched backwards, the shotgun falling from his grasp. This was better than he could have hoped for!

The gun hit the ground and went off with a thunderous blast. The massive discharge from the weapon hit one of the spider wind chimes on the porch and blasted it to pieces.

Up in the hayloft, Tim was struggling to stay hidden. Inside, he was laughing so much he could feel the tears rolling down his cheeks. He watched old Bill Cole banging his fist on the porch in rage.

'I'll get you!' the old man bellowed. 'I'll find you. I know you're the boy from next door!'

The laughter suddenly froze in Tim's throat.

'Aren't you?' Bill Cole continued.

Tim frowned uneasily. But the man couldn't know for sure it was him.

Could he?

'You'll pay for this,' Bill Cole raged. 'No one makes a fool of me! And no one eats my apples!'

'That's what you think,' Tim whispered to himself, and he reached into his bucket and plucked out a large, red, succulent apple. Within seconds, he was down to the core. The little black pips gleamed at him and his gran's words came floating back into his mind.

'Watch out for the pips – don't want a tree growing in your tummy!'

Tim shook his head and smiled. A tree would grow out of his stomach if he swallowed the pips?

'Yeah, right, Gran,' he chuckled.

Outside, he could still hear old Bill Cole ranting and raving. Tim sank back into the straw. He'd shown Bill Cole that he couldn't just bully anyone and get away with it. Then he popped the apple core into his mouth and ate it – pips and all.

Two days had passed since Tim's daring raid on old Bill Cole's orchard. He lay in bed and let the sunlight stream through the crack in the curtains. It was only eight thirty, and he could tell that it was going to be another cloudless, sunny day.

He smiled to himself; leaving the rusty bucket outside the old man's front door, full to the brim with half-eaten fruit, had been a particularly clever idea. He was just sorry he hadn't been able to see old Bill Cole's face when he'd found the bucket. Still, seeing him slip over and shooting the wind chime off the porch had been equally as good. And since then, there hadn't been one sign of the old man coming round to give Gran a hard time either – all in all, a great plan, Tim concluded.

He was rudely interrupted from his thoughts by a shudder running through his body, followed by a loud sneeze.

'Once a wish,' his gran called from downstairs.

Tim got out of bed and stretched.

He sneezed again.

'Twice a kiss,' his gran added, as Tim shook his head and wiped his nose. Surely he wasn't getting a cold? He coughed. A harsh cough that made his whole body shake. He put a hand to his mouth and coughed again.

It felt as if something was stuck in his throat.

He sat on the edge of his bed for a moment longer

and waited for the feeling to pass, and then he got to his feet and wandered into the bathroom.

He ran water into the old porcelain basin and washed his face and hands.

Outside in the yard, Banjo was barking happily. Tim began to think what the two of them could get up to that day.

He had just finished brushing his teeth when he felt the urge to cough once more. Tim was beginning to feel a little uneasy. He rubbed his chest, and coughed yet again.

This time he felt something at the back of his throat.

Something hard and sharp.

He gripped the edge of the sink so hard that he almost overbalanced.

He looked into the mirror over the sink, and stuck out his tongue, his eyes widening in alarm. There were four small, shiny black objects sitting at the back of his mouth – but they were only apple pips.

Tim spat them out and looked at them for a

second, then quickly brushed them into the toilet and flushed them away.

He studied his reflection in the bathroom mirror for a moment longer, satisfied that he didn't look ill, and then he returned to his bedroom and dressed before heading down the stairs for breakfast.

'Another lovely morning,' his gran said as Tim entered the kitchen and sat down. For a moment he wondered whether he should mention what had just happened upstairs, but then he thought better of it and contented himself with tucking into a plate of eggs and bacon.

'Are you feeling all right, Tim? I heard you coughing and sneezing.'

'Oh, that was nothing, Gran,' he replied without looking at her.

'Well, I must say, you certainly *look* well. Your cheeks are as red as apples,' she chuckled.

Tim put his finger to one cheek and, for a second, he was sure that the flesh there felt waxy and smooth – just like the skin of an apple. Suddenly he didn't feel so hungry. He shook his head, telling himself to stop thinking such stupid thoughts, and took another mouthful of food.

'What are you doing with yourself today, then?' Gran enquired.

'Just riding around on my bike and exploring,' he told her, getting to his feet.

'Well, don't go wearing out poor old Banjo, will you? He's not as young as he was. A bit like me.' She smiled and ruffled Tim's hair as he passed her on his way out into the yard.

'Banjo!' he called, waiting for the beagle to come lolloping over to him.

There was no sign of the dog.

'Come on, boy!' Tim urged, walking across the yard towards the barn.

Silence greeted his calls. No excited barks or delighted yapping disturbed the lazy morning solitude of the old farm. Then Tim noticed a dark shape on the far side of the yard near the barn. 'Banjo,' he smiled. 'Come on, I've been calling you.'

Tim walked towards the beagle, a little puzzled to see that the animal was lying on its belly just watching him. Banjo was making no attempt to move towards him. 'Are you all right, boy?' Tim asked, wondering if Banjo was hurt.

When he was within a metre or so of Banjo, the dog got to his feet and bared his teeth. As Tim drew nearer, he began to growl deep in his throat, the sound increasing in volume.

Tim stiffened in surprise. 'What's wrong with you?' he said. 'It's only me.' He extended a hand to the beagle.

Banjo's growl became louder and he began to back away. Tim noticed that the hackles on the back of the beagle's neck were up. The dog barked once then turned and ran, heading off into the overgrown fields beyond the barn.

Tim stood, puzzled and a little worried by Banjo's behaviour. Finally, he climbed on to his bike and rode off across the yard along the dirt track that led away from Gran's farm.

As the day wore on, the sun reached its highest point in the sky and Tim decided that enough was enough. He'd been riding around for hours along the endless networks of dirt tracks he always explored, lost in his own thoughts. Sweat was soaking through his T-shirt. He felt a welcome cool breeze blow across him, and also became aware for the first time of some slight pain from his calves and ankles.

Tim groaned as he glanced down at them and saw the white marks of stinging nettles. He'd been so wrapped up in his own thoughts he hadn't even felt the plants whipping at his legs.

He stopped, snatched up a nearby dock leaf and bent down to rub it on the puffy, itching blots on his calves. As the stinging began to calm, Tim dropped the leaf on the ground and straightened up, anxious to find somewhere cool to rest out of the afternoon heat. But, as he raised his head, he felt a little dizzy. A faint ringing had started in his left ear – a sensation a bit like when he'd been listening to really loud music. Tim wondered if he was going to faint. Maybe he hadn't drunk enough water so far – after all, it was a really hot day. Was he getting sunstroke? Warily, he shook his head, and the ringing faded a little. He got tentatively back on his bike and rode on.

As he entered the yard, there was no sign of Banjo. He cycled across to the barn and propped his bike against the door, sighing in relief as he felt the cool air wafting from inside. He walked in – and gasped as he caught sight of the far wall.

From the eaves, all the way down to the ground, the wall looked as if it had been draped in a thin, greyish-white curtain. It was covered with the gossamer strands of a spider's web.

Fascinated, Tim wandered over to examine the web more closely. The holes between the strands in the enormous web were as big as his fist. He was still inspecting the webs when he became aware of movement to the side of him.

Tim nearly tumbled backwards in shock as a

massive spider hurtled out of the hole closest to him. Without realizing, Tim had leaned too close and brushed against the web.

It was the first time Tim had seen the spider close up. He stared at its swollen, fly-filled abdomen and crawling, hair-covered legs.

The spider began to creep towards the edge of the web. And then, quick as a flash, it dropped to the floor on a thin strand of web and began to scuttle towards Tim.

Unnerved, Tim leaped away and picked up a stone from the floor of the barn, ready to hurl it at the spider. He didn't want to look at it any more.

'Tim!'

The voice made him turn.

Gran was standing in the doorway of the barn. 'What are you doing?' she wanted to know, seeing the stone clutched in his hand.

'There's a spider in here,' he told her. 'A huge one.'

'There's lots of spiders in here, Tim, and don't you

go killing them,' his gran ordered. 'It's bad luck,' she went on. 'You know what they say: if you want to live and thrive, let a spider run alive.'

When Tim looked back, the spider had disappeared back into one of its hiding-places. The web was empty again.

Gran walked over and kissed him on the cheek, and pushed something she'd been holding towards him.

He looked down to see that in his hands was an apple. Tim shuddered.

'Eat that,' she told him, as she walked back towards the house. 'An apple a day keeps the doctor away, that's what they say.'

Gran left him alone in the barn, and Tim dropped the apple on the ground. He didn't even want it in his pocket, let alone in his stomach. Absent-mindedly, he gave his left ear a poke with his finger. An itch had started up deep inside it – the same ear that had been troubling him earlier. The itch remained. Tim shook his head hard, but nothing seemed to help this time. In fact, it seemed to get worse. The itch was joined by a dull rustling noise — like putting his ear to a seashell.

And then it got *much* worse.

It felt like there was a wasp buzzing deep inside Tim's left eardrum — its tiny sting pricking and probing away.

He walked out of the barn, frantically shaking his head and prodding his ear.

Suddenly, Tim became aware that his fingertip was touching something strange in there, bending against his fingertip.

He clamped a hand over the ear, his mind racing, and rushed over to the house and up to the bathroom to peer at his reflection in the mirror.

Turning his head to the right, Tim stared at his left ear. There was something sticking out of it.

Something green and pointed.

Using a finger and thumb, Tim tried to pull the object out, but it was hard to grip and seemed stuck fast.

Tim suddenly felt afraid.

With his heart thumping hard against his ribs, he tried again. This time he managed to get hold of the object. He began to pull.

With an oozing *pop*, the object came free. Tim stared down at it.

It was a leaf.

He stared at the leaf for what felt like a long time.

A leaf . . . in his ear? How had it got there?

Maybe the leaf had fluttered down from a tree as he'd been out riding his bike and landed in his ear. But how could it have got in so deep? It just didn't make sense.

As he stared down at the leaf, Tim heard the ringing sound again. And then the itching started again – but this time it was deep inside his right ear.

Something inside the ear moved.

Tim arched his head round to examine his right ear in the mirror – and nearly cried out in fright. A green furled shape was working its way outwards – twisting and turning towards the light.

Tim's head was spinning and he felt sick. He waited for a moment and calmed himself down a little before leaving the bathroom and wandering outside for some fresh air. First the pips, then Banjo's strange reaction to him, then the spider – and now the leaves! So far, this day had been just *too* weird.

By the time he'd eaten his dinner and watched some TV, Tim felt exhausted.

'Perhaps you *are* coming down with something, love,' Gran said, feeling his forehead. 'Are you *sure* you feel OK?'

For a moment he wondered about mentioning the coughed-up pips and the leaves, but again decided against it. 'I'm just really tired, Gran,' he replied. 'I think I might go up to bed and read for a while before I go to sleep.'

'Good idea,' his gran agreed. 'I'll bring you up some warm milk a bit later.'

'Thanks, Gran,' Tim said, wearily heading for the stairs. He paused at the bottom. 'Have you seen Banjo?'

'He came back for his dinner about an hour ago, but I haven't seen him since,' his gran replied. 'He wouldn't come inside the house for some reason. Silly old dog.' She smiled. 'He waited until I put his food in his bowl out on the porch before he'd eat it. But he'll be back before it starts getting dark – he likes his basket too much!'

Tim nodded and made his way up the stairs into the bathroom. He was just about to pull on his pyjama top, when he felt a large lump in the middle of his stomach. He froze for a second, staring down at this horrific pink addition to his limbs. Tim touched it gently. There was no pain.

He looked more closely, and saw the flesh around the lump shining, as if it was being pushed from the inside. He prodded it again. It was as if someone had stuffed a tennis ball beneath his skin.

And then the lump moved.

Tim shouted out loud. He was breathing quickly now, his mouth was dry, and he could feel acid-like fear rising in the back of his throat.

With shaking fingers, he prodded the lump once more. Again, it moved.

It was beneath his belly-button now. Tim had the strange urge to press against the swelling with both hands. For one terrifying moment, he thought that the skin of his stomach was going to split.

His belly-button opened like a yawning mouth, spat out a round object and closed up again. The object rolled across the floor of the bathroom and, as he saw what it was, Tim let out a terrified scream.

Lying on the floor was a large red apple.

Tim backed away from the gleaming red fruit as if it was a bomb about to explode.

'Tim, are you all right?'

He heard his gran's voice outside the bathroom door but his attention was still riveted on the apple that had emerged from his stomach.

'Tim!' she called again, banging on the door.

Tim looked across at the door, catching a glimpse of his reflection in the bathroom mirror as he did so.

There was another lump on his left shoulder.

This one was smaller, but when Tim raised his hand to touch it, the growth swelled beneath his fingers.

Another was pushing against the flesh on one side of his chest.

Again Gran called to him from the other side of the door.

Tim wanted to call back that he was fine – but he knew that he wasn't. Everything was *far* from fine.

He gripped the edge of the sink as the mirror showed thin tendrils sprouting from his nose and ears.

Like the green shoots of leaves.

'Tim, I want to see if you're all right, love,' Gran insisted, banging on the bathroom door. 'Please!'

Tim leaned nearer to the mirror, his face only centimetres from it. The vision that stared back at him was something from a nightmare.

For a fleeting second, it looked as though the veins in the whites of his eyes had burst. They seemed to swell, spreading across the irises until both eyes turned completely red, as red as the apples in old Bill Cole's orchard.

Feeling light-headed, Tim blinked hard, and found himself looking back into his own eyes again.

What was happening to him?

He reeled away from the mirror and towards the bathroom door. Only one person would know, he was sure of that. Old Bill Cole.

He pulled his T-shirt back on, his hands shaking. Then, tugging open the bathroom door, he hurried past his gran, ignoring her calls, and sprinted downstairs.

He could still hear her calling his name as he dashed out of the front door, but Tim didn't stop. He ran as fast as he could towards the copse of trees, scrambled over the high wall and landed in the orchard. He didn't feel the gorse bushes and the sharp brickwork scratching and cutting at his arms and legs.

He ran as fast as he could in the direction of old

Bill Cole's house. In his haste, he tripped over a fallen branch and went sprawling, narrowly avoiding a collision with a nearby tree.

Panting, Tim levered himself up on the trunk. At first, he thought his eyes were playing tricks on him, but he realized with terrible dread that they weren't.

On the gnarled bark was a face.

The next tree was the same.

And the next.

Every single apple tree around him bore human features. Etched in bark like the nightmare carvings of some mad sculptor.

Tim stared in terror at them. Some were boys. Some were girls. Some had their mouths open as if screaming for help. Several had bulging eyes, the look of horror in those blank wooden orbs showing their fear and desperation.

His head spinning, Tim tried to stagger on towards the farmhouse, but his legs felt heavy. He rested, panting, against a stooped old tree that was more gnarled than the others, and tried to get rid of the dizziness. But then his mouth dropped open in horror and disbelief.

The face on the tree was his grandad's.

Tim tried to scream, but couldn't force the sound out.

He tried again to run, but as he did, he felt something dark and hard tear through the skin of his left forearm. And then his right thigh.

Tim felt no pain, just an awful, grinding, stiffening of his limbs. With a huge effort, he stared wildly down at himself. Jutting from his arms and legs were thick, bark-covered branches.

Suddenly, what looked like a milky-white root burst from his right ankle and burrowed into the earth nearby.

Tim managed to rip his leg forward, but the root flailed around and was joined by others bursting free from his feet.

They rooted Tim to the spot. He tried again to scream for help, but his jaw was now fixed hard. He couldn't turn his head any more. He felt his entire body go rigid, bark forming where flesh had once been.

He heard footsteps nearby.

The figure of old Bill Cole loomed into view directly in front of him. Tim could see that the old man was smiling, watching as the bark began to cover Tim's face.

Terrify yourself with more books from Nick Shadow's
Midnight Library

Vol. V: *Liar*

Lauren is shy. She just wants a friend, and she's so lonely she even imagines herself one. But she soon realizes she's created a monster. A monster called Jennifer . . .

Vol. VI: *Shut your Mouth*

Louise and her mates love to get their sweets from Mr Webster's old-fashioned shop, but when their plan to get some of the new 'Special Delights' goes wrong, could they have bitten off more than they can chew?